★

THERE WAS NOTHING HERE TO SURPRISE KEMP

Everything fitted very logically together, even the manner of Amanda Egerton's death. Yet there was something in Dorothea's reception of it which seemed discordant. On the one hand there had been her obvious distress, but now there was almost relief, as if she'd latched on to the possible cause of her friend's suicide as a desperate way out of some dilemma of her own.

Kemp, fairly used to summing people up without their being aware of it, had not considered Charles's wife to be a person of great complexity, and he would not have observed her so closely now had it not been for his slow realization that, for all her hesitant speech, Dorothea Copeland was herself a watcher, and a careful one....

★

Also available from Worldwide Mysteries by
M.R.D. MEEK

A MOUTHFUL OF SAND
A WORM OF DOUBT
THE SPLIT SECOND
IN REMEMBRANCE OF ROSE
HANG THE CONSEQUENCES

A Forthcoming Worldwide Mystery by
M.R.D. MEEK

THIS BLESSED PLOT

A LOOSE CONNECTION
M.R.D. MEEK

WORLDWIDE®

TORONTO • NEW YORK • LONDON • PARIS
AMSTERDAM • STOCKHOLM • HAMBURG
ATHENS • MILAN • TOKYO • SYDNEY

A LOOSE CONNECTION

A Worldwide Mystery/April 1991

This edition is reprinted by arrangement with Charles Scribner's Sons; an imprint of Macmillan Publishing Company.

ISBN 0-373-26070-9

A LOOSE CONNECTION

M.R.D. MEEK

ONE

'I'VE GOT SOMETHING to tell you, Freckles.' Amanda's voice on the telephone was pitched high with excitement, and it jabbed at the edge of Dorothea's headache like a steel bolt.

'Don't call me Freckles,' she said in the colourless monotone she used nowadays when she talked to Mandy. 'What is it you've got to tell me?' Even after all these years curiosity could still catch her out, betray her into asking, so deep and of such long-standing was the interest she had in her friend's peculiar lifestyle—peculiar that is to Dorothea, who didn't have one.

'Oh, I can't possibly tell you on the phone.' Mandy sounded her usual hectic self, the words tumbling over each other. 'It's the weirdest thing, Dot... Something you'll never believe... Meet me tomorrow for lunch and I'll tell you.'

'I'm sorry, Mandy, it's my Save the Children morning...'

'Save them another day. I simply have to see you. Something's come up... from a long way back. Only you will understand. And if I don't get it out, I'll burst!' Mandy's gurgling laugh came across the line, warm and intimate as if she was standing in the same room. 'Do come tomorrow, Dottie, you can get another of your do-gooding ladies to mind the store.'

As she hesitated, a hand pressed tight to her throbbing temple, Dorothea thought of all the times she had given in, trailed faithfully in the wake of that splendid effervescent spirit which bore Amanda along like a bubble on the surface of a millrace, splendid and unscathed.

'I don't know if I can manage it. I should be at the shop. We're all volunteers you know, and it's not fair if one of us drops out.' How dull her explanation sounded, how faltering her excuses. 'If it were something important...'

'But this *is* important. Terribly important,' Mandy broke in. 'And anyway, it's ages since we met. Aren't you in the least curious as to what I have to tell you?'

She's probably got a new man. That's all it is. Mandy always did have that febrile note in her voice when she was on the brink of a fresh adventure. And how avidly I used to listen, and watch the golden-brown eyes sparkle, and the soft pink lips curl round his name, his status, his possessions!

But this time I don't think I want to know. Mandy's life has taken her far from mine, there's no bridge any more, we might as well be in different worlds instead of her in London and me out here in Newtown, not thirty miles away.

'No, I'm not that curious, Mandy,' she heard herself say.

'But it concerns you too. Didn't you hear what I said? It's like something out of a film or one of those television sagas...'

Of course it would be larger than life, or dramatized to make it so. All Mandy's tales were like that; fables to which she had exclusive wizardry. Half of Dorothea yearned to respond as she had always done, the other half simply wanted to take her headache upstairs and cherish it in the darkened peace it so insistently demanded.

'Well,' she said, not softening the querulous note, 'if it's all that important, why not tell me now?'

'Not on the telephone.' Mandy's voice sank to a whisper. 'I can't possibly tell you this on the phone. Do come tomorrow, Freckles.' She was wheedling now. 'The usual place. Half-twelve. That suits your train, doesn't it?'

Weariness intervened, compliance easier than to prolong the conversation. 'Oh, all right, then. Lunch at the usual place. Look, Mandy, I must go... I've got the most awful headache.'

'Poor old Freckles. You still get them?' Mandy's ready commiseration was genuine enough, the effect spoiled as she went on: 'I've never had a headache in my life. See you tomorrow. And, Dot? What I have to tell you will blow your mind free of any headache. 'Bye...'

Dorothea put the phone down, went to her immaculate kitchen for a glass of water, swallowed her tablets and slowly climbed the stairs. Lucky Mandy, never getting headaches... Of course they called them migraines now but Dorothea hadn't found it made the pain any easier to bear.

What on earth had made Amanda so excited this time? Something out of the past, she'd said. Well, that covered at least twenty years. Something that would blow her mind... Surely that expression was dead as the dodo, dead as the 'sixties? Stupid to use it now... They were no longer girls, she and Mandy.

Dorothea lay down, carefully pushing aside the duvet. The pillow under her head was blessedly cool. She closed her eyes, and hoped the pills would act quickly. She must be better by the time Charley got home, otherwise it was not fair to him. She was swept by an overwhelming sense of guilt which she accepted without surprise; a state of guilt seemed to be chronic—like her headaches—and she never questioned why that should be so.

Dorothea stirred, restlessly. She found herself resenting Amanda's easy temperament that threw off yesterday as casually as last season's fashion. She's come through unscathed, she thought, that's what Mandy's done. 'Life's a bowl of cherries,' she'd said once, flaunting its quality in

Dorothea's face, 'spit out the stones, and pick another bunch...'

All right for her. Dorothea was drifting off into oblivion. She heard Amanda's voice again: 'Trouble with you, Freckles, you were born with a sense of sin and you've never shaken it off...'

TWO

LENNOX KEMP in his office at Gillorns, Solicitors of Newtown, looked irritably at the list on the desk in front of him. Accounts were not his favourite pastime. Only polite, but persistent calls from Head Office had eventually forced him to give attention to the document. He was in charge of this branch of the firm and therefore responsible for all matters pertaining to it but the task of scrutinizing the costs of the various departments under his wing was one he viewed with less than joy.

'We're in the black,' he'd complained to his secretary, Elvira, when she'd plumped the papers on his desk, and relayed the gist of the overtures from Clements Inn. 'What more do they want?'

'A breakdown of the figures, Mr Kemp, and your comments.'

'Who's doing well, and who isn't?' he said, gloomily. 'Reminds me of old Macready when he used to try and chop me down on expenses...'

'That was a long time ago, Mr Kemp. And it was Mrs Macready who did the accounts—and the chopping.'

'With overmuch of her vaunted Scottish shrewdness,' he agreed, 'but she had a motherly bosom and made good scones...'

Elvira grinned down at him. They had both come far since those sleazy days in Walthamstow but she was glad he remembered. Kemp then had been out of his profession—struck off by the Law Society, in fact—and reduced to earning his crusts on the underside of the legal world as an operative in Macready's Detective Agency where she'd worked as a typist.

'I don't think either Mr Pilgrim or Mr Abott have motherly or any other sort of bosoms,' she said pertly, 'more like full metal jackets, those two, under their pinstripes... They've phoned for these figures every day for a week.'

'You know, Elvira,' Kemp reflected, 'we're in danger of having our lives run by accountants. They're a new breed of vulture... Oh well, leave it with me. I'll try and give them their money's worth—or else you and I might find ourselves walking down those mean streets again, eh?'

Elvira laughed as she closed the door behind her. No fear of that; Lennox Kemp, now reinstated as a solicitor, was too highly regarded by his present firm, and her fortunes had risen with his.

All the same, she guessed that there were times when he hankered for the old excitements, and for the closer contacts he'd had with the realities beneath the surface on that lower level of society where folk live perilously on the criminal fringe, and where he had exercised his talent for unorthodox investigation. Although he had salvaged his reputation and attained a measure of respectability, a waywardness still lurked in him which would not wholly accept the status quo or the strictures it put upon him.

Like this business of having to comment on the monthly costs reaped by his colleagues in the branch... It offends his sense of fairness, Elvira thought, as she clicked her high heels down the corridor to the typists' room, and it's just that sense of fairness in Mr Kemp which keeps this office running smoothly. She wondered how long he would take to go through the figures; she reckoned he'd be much happier if he had a murder case to brood over...

Kemp swivelled his chair away from his desk and looked out of the window. The skyline of Newtown on a dull day in January was not an inspiring sight, but then neither were the papers on his desk. He lit a cigarette and thought about them.

Of course Head Office—or, more particularly, the financial stormtroopers who were manfully leading it from the rear—were right to want reassurance. There were salaries to be considered, pensions provided for, loans serviced and bank managers comforted; the bills for heating, lighting and equipment must be paid else a nuclear winter might descend and all work grind to a halt. Such facts were so universal as to have become mere platitudes.

Weighed in that balance the Newtown Branch was on the side of the angels, for it was highly profitable. In the few years since the old firm in the City had thought it expedient to open up here in the outback of the Metropolis, Gillorns of Newtown had proved a very successful venture. Nor did it lack the competitive spirit so beloved of modern economic man. Without being too brash and thrusting in this new era of blatant advertisement, Gillorns' reputation for giving honest service at a sensible price had put them well ahead of any local rivals... God, thought Kemp, whose mind was running on these lines, I'm beginning to think like a grocer! Which was in fact exactly what he had once been told by his principal when he was an articled clerk: 'We're in the market dispensing expert legal advice and people should buy it over the counter like packets of tea, so we can't ignore Smithers' Stores up the road where the tea might be dust but the prices are rock-bottom.'

This sound commercial concept was not one that had been popular in the 'sixties with many of Kemp's fellow students, who saw themselves in the future manning Legal Aid centres and assisting the unfortunate—an idealistic fancy which had ended in tears before bedtime just as Nanny had predicted. Nevertheless, Kemp whose attitude to life was more or less to accept the rough with the smooth, had firmly attached the concept to the back of his mind. Consequently its fervent propagation in the stern 'eighties came as no real surprise although it was not in his nature to accord it any ecstatic welcome.

Competition with other firms was all very well, but competition within his own branch he found distasteful, so he eyed the list of costs now on his desk with wary hostility. Only the increasing volume of business had overcome his initial objection to splitting the Branch up into rigid departments and he still liked to think that any one of his colleagues could take over anybody else's work in an emergency—so long as that emergency was not prolonged.

This meant that Michael Cantley, their maestro before the magistrates, had to learn to tone down his cultivated assertiveness when faced with the bereaved seeking probate, and that young Lambert, so confident in a tricky conveyancing matter, must occasionally raise his head in Court though he said he'd rather put it in a bucket. His assistant, Charles Copeland, could not exercise such versatility being a legal executive, but Charley could be called upon at any time to tackle anyone's paperwork with more careful attention to the duller details which his professionally qualified colleagues were inclined to skip.

Even Nick Stoddart, whose high opinion of his own prowess in the field of civil litigation was a self-inflicted malady and a constant irritation to others, had at times of special stress to buckle down to drafting leases to cover every eventuality from acts of God to frying-pan fires.

And, because tax considerations flowed under everything like leaking subsoil, Sally Stacey was always in demand since making a quiet niche for herself as an expert in Revenue law, and guardian of that sacred fount.

All in all, they made a good team, and Kemp had no desire to see discord among them, and he feared that this newfangled notion from Head Office that competitive costings should be monitored might well sow the seeds of internecine conflict.

Kemp sighed; his not to reason why.

He bent to his task, mouthing the names and figures as if they were commodities on the Stock Exchange.

Divorce and allied matrimonials several points up—a rise to cause concern among moralists or social scientists but gratifying to accountants. Legal aid was showing a good dividend, if tardily; the Country Court tax-masters were fair if you didn't try and go over the top. Neither Kemp nor his assistant, Perry Belchamber, had reason to complain.

Criminal costs were also rising—possibly due to an increase in nefarious activities during the winter months which favoured the cunning at the expense of the careless. His friend Inspector John Upshire mightn't be too pleased unless it meant they'd caught more villains. Pity Mr Cantley never got the chance to prosecute nowadays; always appearing for the defence tended to blunt his rhetorical skill, and he complained that he was fast running out of pleas in mitigation.

Shares in civil suits remained steady and were probably at a higher figure than their real worth. Kemp could only just tolerate Nick Stoddart, who had been recommended by Head Office for his vast experience and negotiating flair; so far Kemp had seen evidence of neither.

Costs in probate were healthy, even taking an upward trend. Surely not a reflection on the death-rate in Newtown? More likely it showed the populace were more knowledgeable and property-conscious in the present climate. Several large estates had been settled recently, and the department had the benefit of some solid trust work handed over by Archie Gillorn, the senior partner at Clements Inn, when he retired. Mr Lambert preferred trust and probate to the hurly-burly of the commercial world, so he tended to leave most of the conveyancing to Charles Copeland.

Kemp stared at the figures for this last department; they had taken a sharp tumble. Not to put too fine a point upon it, the fall was disastrous.

This was the reason, then, for all the panic. Conveyancing, once the mainstay of the suburban practice—some said, its bread-and-butter—had been hit initially by competition from the High Street agencies but that was an old story by now. Things had settled down since the first impact, business had rallied, and this should have shown as an upsurge in the figures. Instead, they had plunged to a new low.

Kemp couldn't understand it. Conveyancing ought to be quietly lucrative in a place like Newtown where people were always on the move—wasn't that what new towns were all about? London-based firms housed their workers here, and a natural mobility, engendered by the prosperous industrial estates surrounding the town, meant that young people went from first to second homes, three-bedroomed to four, as their families and ambitions expanded.

He got out the records for previous months. The decline had been a gradual one with the sharpest fall the most recent. He still couldn't understand it. Unlike other departments where earnings rarely materialized until cases were closed and accounts rendered—the inevitable delay between performance and reward—costs incurred in the buying and selling of property jogged along at the rate of the work done, being merely extracted from moneys available on completion. Lowered takings therefore simply signified lack of business. But why should there be such a lack? There was plenty of business about . . .

Kemp liked Charles Copeland whom he considered a decent man, a keen worker, if perhaps rather colourless in personality. He'd been with Gillorns since he left school, first as an office boy, then, by dint of night-school study and examination success, he'd become a qualified legal executive, and had already reached the highest level possible for him at the Clements Inn office before coming out to Newtown. His competence and integrity had by then become a byword in the firm, and Kemp had been fortunate in getting Charles to move to the branch three years ago.

Now it was clear that something was going wrong.

Kemp was still frowning over the papers when Elvira brought him mid-morning coffee. She glanced down.

'You look worried, Mr Kemp.'

'I am.'

'It's Charley's figures, isn't it?' Elvira had wide experience of costings, and anyway it was she who had typed the list.

'You never listen to office gossip, do you?'

Kemp gave her a sharp look.

'I try not to hear it.'

'You never despised it in other offices when you used to be working on cases... Chatting up the typists and the cleaners gave you the worm's eye view—that's what you used to say.'

'Quite a different kettle of fish. As an inquiry agent I was in a scurvy trade. Solicitors are supposed to be above that kind of thing.' He realized how he sounded, and that Elvira had a hand over her mouth to hide her amusement. 'Come on then, Miss Big Ears, what have you got to tell me?'

She hesitated. 'It's about Charley...'

It threw an interesting sidelight on office mores that whereas the staff referred to the solicitors as Mr So-and-so, Charles Copeland was always Charley to them.

'Go on.'

'Well, I did some letters the other day for Mr Stoddart because his Doreen was off sick. When I took them in to him he had a client but Mr Stoddart asked me to wait while he signed the letters. He has this habit of going on talking at the same time as he's signing—just to show he's capable of doing two things at once...' Had Elvira not aspired to a ladylike demeanour she might have given a contemptuous sniff. 'Anyway, this client was saying he had a new block of flats going up and could Gillorns take on the legal work when it came to selling the individual units. Mr Stoddart went all evasive like, inferring that our conveyancing department wasn't up to it ... Of course he wrapped it up in that airy-fairy way he has, but that was his meaning, plain enough to me, and surely plain to the client ...'

Kemp was staring at her.

'Did you know this client, Elvira?'

'Yes, it was Mr Begg from Brown Brothers. We've done a lot of work for them. I couldn't understand it. It sounded just as if Mr Stoddart was turning away work from Charley's department.'

Kemp was silent for a moment.

'There may be other reasons, Elvira,' he said, cautiously. 'It would be wrong to jump to conclusions. But I will look into it.' He gave her a sudden grin. 'And do stop reminding me about the old days. I'm doing my best to forget them... Now would you ask Mr Lambert if he can spare me a moment?'

Tony Lambert had the kind of youthful features, snub nose, rounded chin and wide-apart eyes, that never age, so he wore enormous glasses to counter the effect; they only made him look more than ever like an over-earnest sixthformer.

'Oh, I see you've got these figures out at last,' he said now, settling in the chair opposite Kemp. 'No worries, I hope?'

Kemp turned the list in his direction.

'Only Charles Copeland's.'

Tony looked at the paper, and poked at his spectacles with a forefinger, a nervous habit he had when needing time to think.

'Yes ... I see.'

'Well?'

'Not very good, are they?'

'They're disastrous. I was hoping you could give me a reason for them.'

Tony looked uncomfortable. 'Charley's been working that department on his own. I thought that was the arrangement you made. I didn't realize they were down so far...'

'But you knew something was wrong?'

'I've realized that for some time, Lennox. Things haven't been going well for Charles lately. Surely you've noticed?'

'Noticed what?'

Tony shifted his long legs. 'Well... there's been an atmosphere. How can I put it?'

'Succinctly, I hope.'

Lambert removed his spectacles, put them on the desk, and looked at Kemp with large grey guileless eyes.

'It started about six months ago. Do you mean to say you didn't know?'

'Know what?' Kemp was beginning to get exasperated.

'Well, perhaps you wouldn't. You're out of the office a lot, and anyway you were on holiday when Nick Stoddart first arrived.'

'You mean there's something going on between Nick Stoddart and Charles?'

Tony nodded. 'They knew each other back at Head Office. We all reckoned that there must have been some kind of trouble... Apparently they never got on well, and now Nick's here working in Newtown it seems to have come to the surface.'

'In what way?'

Tony tapped his glasses on the desk, and looked out of the window.

'I need to know, Tony.' Kemp put it gently.

'Nick all but ignores Charley. He rarely speaks to him, and when he does it's with that lordly tone he uses when he wants to bring people down a peg. He's really quite unfair... and you know Charley, he's a bit thin-skinned, and anyway how can he answer back—in his position?'

'Oh Lord, spare me the class struggle!' It was said half-jokingly but it betrayed Kemp's anger at what he'd just heard. 'Do you think this attitude of Nick's is affecting Charley's work, because that's what we're here to discuss?'

'I can only guess. But, yes, I think if I were in Charley's shoes I'd be blistering mad. It's a rotten thing in an office of this size when there's personal antagonism but it's much worse when one of them's in a subordinate position.'

Kemp sat back and thought for a moment.

'I'm glad you've opened up on this, Tony. I never realized what was going on. I'll admit I was rather surprised that Nick came to us at all. He seems to me the type who likes to be at the centre of the action, not out here on the frontier.'

Tony gave a wry smile. 'If you want my opinion, Lennox, I think the people at Clements Inn wanted rid of our Mr Stoddart. The way he throws his weight about, I'm not surprised.'

'You think they off-loaded him on to us?'

'Something like that.' Lambert resumed his glasses, and with them, his expression of high-minded seriousness. 'I shouldn't be gossiping like this. Only, I thought you knew...'

'This isn't gossip, Tony. It's a question of office morale. And I won't have Charles Copeland put down by anybody. I've never had complaints about his work, and he's a loyal member of the staff. Have you any idea what happened between him and Nick back there in the London office?'

'I don't know anything specific...' Tony was fiddling with his glasses again. 'I still see Nigel Crawford occasionally when I'm up in Town. He took over from Stoddart. I did ask Nigel if he knew what the trouble was. He was a bit vague, but apparently it dates from a long way back. Stoddart was articled about the time Charley started at Gillorns—they're both about the same age—so they've known each other for ages...'

'But that must be twenty years ago! You'd still be at kindergarten when Charles and Stoddart started out on their legal careers—not to mention yours truly as a greenhorn of twenty-three just down from University and thinking of the Law as an honourable pursuit... God, you do make me feel middle-aged!' He watched Tony's discomfiture with amusement. 'All right, leave this to me. I'll try and straighten things out with Charley first, but not here in the office with twenty pairs of pointed ears. I'll invite him out for a drink one evening, then I'll tackle Stoddart—who's not the easiest man to talk to.'

Lambert rose to go. 'I keep well out of his way,' he said, fervently, 'he's senior to me, and by Jove, doesn't he make that clear...'

Kemp narrowed his eyes. 'So that's how the land lies. Well, if I find cause, I'll deal with Mr Stoddart on my terms. I don't need to tell you to keep this under your hat, Tony. Our job in this office is to sort out our clients' problems—and in an imperfect world there's plenty there to keep us occupied—not indulge in petty little squabbles of our own.'

Sometimes Kemp wondered if management was quite his metier—running other people's lives when he hadn't been altogether successful at running his own. Here he was, over forty and unmarried, professionally intact to be sure, but still prone to be drawn into trouble by an inveterate curiosity which looked at sleeping dogs with such a wary eye that they woke barking round his feet.

He just hoped that this particular contretemps could be quietly disposed of without anyone's head rolling into the basket.

THREE

THE RESTAURANT at the top of the Regent Street store was already crowded when Dorothea arrived but Amanda waved to her from a window table. The assembled customers gave the impression of being penguins adrift on an ice floe, black and white being the fashionable colours this season. But Amanda Egerton was in gun-metal grey with creamy guipure lace at her neck and a scarlet chiffon scarf flaming like a beacon on her short black hair.

Mandy always did have the trick with scarves, thought Dorothea moodily as she threaded her way among the tables. Dorothea herself had never mastered it; on her they looked either plainly peasant or slovenly suburban.

'I got here early. Simply couldn't wait.' Amanda brushed her friend's cheek lightly, breathing warmth and subtle perfume. Dorothea's was eau-de-Cologne, and toilet water at that.

'Lovely to see you, Freckles.'

'Don't call me that,' said Dorothea automatically. 'You know nobody calls me that any more.'

'Well, I do. And you've still got them. How long is it since we met?'

'It must be over six months. You'd just got back from your Greek holiday.'

'As long ago as that?' For Mandy, Greece was already a faded memory. 'But I've phoned you often. I do keep in touch.' She said it with complacency as if bestowing a modest favour. In fact she actually saw it as such. She was studying the menu. 'Thank God this place does a decent ladies' lunch. I'm sick of foreign food—and that includes

American. They can't have a nice day unless it includes a steak or two.'

They ordered. Mandy asked for a glass of white wine, Dorothea a dry sherry; she rarely drank alcohol except when lunching with Mandy.

'You've been back to the States, then?'

'New York last autumn and purely on business. But that's not what I have to tell you...' Mandy was a designer in the fashion trade, a career she took seriously but rarely talked about, which irritated Dorothea who had no career of her own, and was therefore intensely curious about the nuts and bolts of the commercial world. She would dearly love to know, for instance, such mundane things as Mandy's actual earnings and what she paid in tax. Mandy always seemed to have plenty of money, but there had been that friendly divorce from the shadowy Derek which was supposed to have brought in a handsome settlement. Brooding sometimes, Dorothea would reflect on how little she knew of her friend's life, not the high style of it, but the basic details, the small essentials which ruled Dorothea's day to day existence so inexorably. It was not that Mandy was consciously reticent on the subject of her work, simply that she dismissed it as routine and therefore not worth talking about when there were more exciting things in life.

Mandy was forking up her salad greedily, pushing the shreds of lettuce into her mouth with rosy-tipped fingers, drinking, not sipping her wine, calling for another glass, chattering merrily. She goes through her food like a fish through plankton, thought Dorothea, only toying with hers. Does she gobble up her men like that, too? She watched Amanda's short upper lip moving, that short upper lip which is so attractive when the teeth behind it are not too large and give it a rabbity look... Mandy's teeth were pearls, small, white and even.

But for all her inconsequential chatter, Mandy knew the form, she kept to the rules of conversation. First, you asked for your friend's health, inquired about her husband and her home, her son and his wellbeing. Yes, answered Dorothea dutifully: Charley is fine, so is Ian, and yes, he's at college and likes it... Is Mandy probing for disasters? Well, thankfully, there are none. I'm being unfair... She really is interested in other people, even if their lives are as humdrum as mine. It's part of her charm. She felt a rush of affection for her friend, and meeting the gold-flecked eyes which couldn't suppress excitement, Dorothea finally gave a wide receptive smile.

'Come on, then. Out with it. You're obviously dying to tell me.'

Amanda pushed her plate aside.

'Let's skip the sweet,' she said. 'We'll have lots of coffee and a couple of brandies. Yes, two Armagnacs, please, and a pot of coffee...'

When the waiter had gone she plumped her elbows on the table, and turned a glowing face to her companion.

'This thing I've got to tell you about, it deserves a proper setting. There ought to be music... Maybe a whole orchestra rising from the floor!'

Dorothea couldn't help laughing. Really, Mandy was quite incorrigible.

'It's a celebration, then?' Perhaps Mandy was going to get married again. That would make it the third time.

Amanda had small, seemingly boneless hands, like puppies' paws, and much given to gesticulation, but now she clasped them in front of her and took a deep breath.

'No, I don't really think it's anything to celebrate, at least not where you and I are concerned. But we ought to share in it because it's out of the past of both of us.'

'I can hardly wait,' said Dorothea drily.

Amanda looked at her with wide, solemn eyes, her levity for the moment stilled as though she wasn't sure of its place.

'I've seen someone, Dottie. Somebody we thought was dead.'

The waiter brought their tray of coffee, set out the cups and the small glasses of dark amber liquor. 'I've not had this before,' said Dorothea, admiring hers. 'It looks nice. Who's this person you've seen?'

'Do you remember Queenie? Queenie Mangan?'

'Of course I do. She ran that horrible office where you and I first met. She was the bane of our young lives, that woman, until she died in that dreadful accident.'

'Right on all counts...except that she didn't die in the fire... And why did you say accident? Unlike you, Dorothea, not to remember. It was a fire.'

Dorothea was staring at her. 'Of course Queenie died. They found her body. There was an inquest.'

'She didn't die.' Mandy's face was flushed, pink on white, and the glass in her hand trembled as she raised it to her lips. A drop glistened at the corner of her mouth as she replaced her drink carefully on the cloth. 'Queenie is alive and well, and living in some style.'

'But that's impossible, Mandy. How do you know this?'

'Because I've seen her...'

'Someone who looked like her. Oh, do be sensible. It's nearly twenty years ago!'

'I know as well as you do how long it's been. But it wasn't someone like her. It was Queenie. And, guess who she was with?'

'I'm past guessing. And anyway, I simply don't believe you.'

Dorothea picked up her drink and took a gulp, choking on it as her throat constricted.

'Let me tell you, then...' That was the way Mandy had always begun one of her flights of fancy. 'I'll tell 'ee a tale...' This would be just another of them.

'Last weekend Clive and I were at that place in the Cotswolds where they have the most gorgeous food—'

'Who's Clive?'

'Oh, nobody who matters. It's got nothing to do with Clive.' Amanda dismissed him with a flutter of fingers. 'He's not important. Anyway, came Sunday lunch and we were in the dining-room partaking of the gastronomic delights it's famous for when I saw this couple at another table. Well, actually it was her voice I heard first. Could you ever forget that voice? Though I must admit her accent's improved no end. I couldn't believe it, thought I must be dreaming... Not that I'd ever waste my time dreaming of that creature. I simply had to turn around and take a closer look. It was Queenie all right. Aged, of course, but haven't we all?'

'Mandy, after twenty years lots of middle-aged women could look like Queenie...'

'Ah, but her companion...' Mandy drained her drink, and paused to give her next revelation its full effect. 'It was her companion who clinched it. It was him who made it so sensational. Dorothea—are you listening?—the man with Queenie was the Major himself. Our erstwhile beloved boss, Bulett the Bold!'

There was a chill in Dorothea's stomach, which was the opposite of what brandy was supposed to do to you. A hard lump was forming there like a snowball. She hurried to drink some coffee, and spluttered.

'It couldn't be...'

'Why ever not? *He* didn't die. And there was no mistaking the back of his head. Straight up like a block of wood. Not so much hair but the same carroty colour. And he still has that same stout—er—military bearing he was so proud of, and the same piggy eyes, I'll be bound, though I didn't get around to seeing them. Now, do you understand why I was so anxious to tell you—you of all people?'

But Dorothea didn't want to understand. Dorothea wanted desperately to dismiss the whole thing as just another figment of Mandy's fertile imagination.

'You're making it up,' she said ungenerously, mopping spilt coffee from her knuckles.

'Why should I make it up?' Mandy exploded. 'I saw them both with my own eyes—in broad daylight. And, there's more...'

'Go on. Did you approach them, talk to them?'

'Don't be daft. They didn't see me. But I went past for a closer look. Told Clive I was going to the loo. Then I skipped out to reception and checked the visitors' book. You're never going to credit this—they'd booked in as Major and Mrs Bulett. And it was his signature. I'm not likely to have forgotten that, the number of times I'd seen it...' She stopped, and when her eyes met Dorothea's, they were serious. 'Dottie, she married him!'

'The register entry wouldn't signify anything,' said Dorothea tartly, 'after all, you're not married to this Clive person and I'll bet you signed in as man and wife...'

'That's different,' said Mandy airily, 'but those other two, Queenie and the Major, they even looked married.'

Dorothea was silent. The discomfort in her gut was growing, she felt rising nausea. I'm being affected by Mandy again, she thought; she always had this ability to raise my temperature, quicken my heart-beat.

Mandy went on talking. 'Luckily, Clive and I were leaving immediately after lunch so I didn't have to see them again or I don't know what I'd have done. Probably waltzed over and said something silly like "How lovely to see you again, Queenie, I thought you were dead..."' There was mischief behind Amanda's eyes despite their solemnity.

'It's really true,' Dorothea said dully. 'You really did see Queenie Mangan. She's alive...' She shivered. 'But it's impossible, Mandy. You remember how certain the police were, all those inquiries they made. And there was a positive identification—they found that bracelet of hers.'

'Yes, I remember. And I've done a lot of thinking about it these last few days. There was the forensic evidence at the inquest. It was the body of a female in her thirties, Queenie was missing... She'd no people of her own. Well, come to think of it, who'd ever want to own up to being kin to Queenie? And the clothes were hers—what was left of them stuck to the ghastly remains—'

'Stop it, Mandy!'

Amanda shrugged. 'Oh, come off it, Freckles, we all talked about it at the time, and you weren't so squeamish then. You were as keen as anybody to discuss the gory details. Don't you remember the terrible fascination it had for us? We couldn't stop talking about it. You and I, Mr Seymour our poor old put-upon cashier, the typists, and even that ragtag bunch of down-and-outs old Bulett called his sales force! And Larry, of course, though he never had much to say on the subject somehow—which was a change for him. You surely haven't forgotten Larry the Lamb?'

'I've forgotten them all. It was so long ago,' Dorothea muttered defensively. She must get things into proportion. It was coming at her too fast... 'Yes, I suppose we did talk about it a lot. We were only about seventeen then...'

Amanda poured herself out more coffee. Her hand poised over Dorothea's cup. Dorothea shook her head. She bent down to retrieve her handbag, and to let the blood flow back into her cheeks for she was sure they had drained of colour.

'I have to go. My train...'

'You can't just leave! Dottie, for heaven's sake...haven't you been listening to what I've said?'

Dorothea was drawing on her gloves, smoothing them over her wedding ring. She could not rid herself of the sick feeling; it must have been that brandy stuff.

'Yes, I've listened. But I still don't believe it. All right, you may have seen Major Bulett with someone who resembles Queenie. Look, Mandy, I had a bad migraine yesterday. It's left me a bit washed out.'

'Oh, they're migraines now, are they?' But Mandy's warm smile took out any sting that might be imagined behind the words. Why do I have to keep criticizing her, thought Dorothea, responding to the smile? But she knew it was in her nature to do so. She was suddenly aware of their long friendship, so close in those early years and still a bond between them. Exasperating as Mandy could be, thoughtless sometimes, yet touchingly vulnerable when her impulsive yearning for adventure led her into trouble, she had that special gift which could bind people to her. She's like a lamp, Dorothea was thinking, and that's what she was to me the first day she came into that dreadful place, she lit up its dreariness, the shabby realities I couldn't go on facing without her...

'You think I'm making a big thing out of this, Dottie.' Mandy leant forward, her face serious. She too could read her friend like an open book, ever since that first day; even Dorothea's freckles hadn't changed. Now she was pale, they stood out. 'But I do think it's important. You must see the implications—you of all people.'

'If it's true...'

'Of course it's true. I'm not a complete idiot. I did see both Major Bulett and Queenie Mangan as was. She wasn't a ghost. She was sitting there large as life eating salmon trout like a lady.'

Dorothea giggled, though she put her hand to her mouth as if it were an indiscretion. 'I can't imagine Queenie ever being a lady,' she said, 'nor can I see her married to the Major. Why, he didn't even like her.'

'Well, she is, and anyway, liking has nothing much to do with marriage.'

'You should know, Mandy, after all your experience.'

'Spoken like a good old trooper, Freckles.' Mandy never took offence at such remarks, treating them as her due. 'And do you remember what you used to say about those two?'

'I've no idea,' said Dorothea warily, 'it was such a long time ago.'

'So you keep saying. What you used to say was that you thought Queenie had a hold over our boss. You said she was blackmailing him.'

'Mandy, we said a lot of silly things in those days. We gossiped like mad about anything and everybody in that office. It was all we had to talk about when we worked there.'

'But, don't you see, perhaps you were right. Perhaps she forced him to marry her...'

'He already had at least two wives living at the time, and no divorce that we could see,' said Dorothea curtly, and then was appalled; she had slipped into the way they used to talk. 'The one he lived with, and that other one—where was it?—in Newcastle? Remember how we got those awful phone calls which he wouldn't answer? That damned switchboard you and I were supposed to look after, with the dolls' eyes falling about and the terrible ringing we couldn't stop? And we kept making mistakes and cutting off his important calls, and he'd come storming out...'

'Well, he told us to cut the calls from Newcastle but we had to listen before we knew what they were... Oh, Mandy, what a dreadful place that was to work in!'

But Mandy was off on another tack.

'One thing I never understood about that night—the night of the fire—was why you were so positive Queenie was there late.'

'She always worked late—everyone else said so too.'

'But you were so sure, Dot. I remember how we stood out there the next morning. I got there before you. There were the firemen, and the police, and all the staff huddled together not knowing what to do, and the Major striding up and down telling everybody to keep calm as if it was a battlefield instead of just the office burning down! And you came off the bus at the corner as you always did, and you saw the crowd...'

Dorothea remembered vividly, though she'd rather she didn't. She'd tried to keep it out of her head for so long... Her heels click-clacking on the pavement, then slowing as the terrible feeling of apprehension grew. She'd seen the shell of the building, smoke still rising, the tangle of hosepipes, the wet road outside, the splayed timbers of the doorway leaning crooked across the entrance where they all used to go in, chattering, every morning at a quarter to nine.

'I'd already found out what had happened from Mr Seymour,' Mandy was saying, 'he said they thought it started after eleven o'clock. And I told you, and the first thing you said was "Queenie"... Don't you remember?'

'How do you expect me to remember? It's twenty years ago, Mandy,' Dorothea burst out in sudden anger. Then, aware of Amanda's bright, knowing eyes upon her, she swallowed and went on levelly. 'I wasn't the only one to think of Queenie. Everyone knew she was working late that week. Queenie liked to impress the firm that she could run it on her own, and one of the Directors was due down from Derby in a few days. She'd want to have all the facts and figures at her fingertips to show how clever she was...'

There was some hint of admiration in her friend's eyes. 'But you could do that too, Dorothea, if they'd have given you the chance. What do they call it, an almost photographic memory? You were the one who could always find things, even when we lost the invoices deliberately behind the radiators.' Mandy was laughing at the memory. 'And when we made mistakes you were the one who reminded us to change the stock records before we got found out. Mind you, Larry was a help there...'

'Larry was your pigeon, Mandy, you had him under your thumb.'

'Larry was easy. Such a handsome brute, with his brains in his boots. Do you remember the day you got your shorthand wrong and we sent that load of vacuum cleaners to the

North of Scotland instead of just round the corner to Thorpe's?'

Dorothea felt herself flushing. Even after all this time she hated being reminded of mistakes.

'I was rushed off my feet with work, and I had a headache that day. I couldn't see straight...' But she could now, she could see clearly that outline she'd taken for 'Thurso' instead of 'Thorpe's... She was aware that Mandy was laughing, just as she'd laughed at the time.

'Oh, Freckles, my dear, what does it matter now? Although Queenie would have got you sacked on the spot, everybody hated her guts so much they covered up. What fun it was! Larry got the consignment back, and even old Seymour agreed to alter the delivery notes. And we ganged up on Queenie, and made her swear not to tell Bulett...'

'She took it out on me afterwards, though. She was really nasty.' Old resentment flared up in Dorothea, making her voice shake.

'She certainly picked on you more than the rest of us. And you were too sensitive. Thank God, the fire meant we all got our books. Doesn't that expression date one, Dot? As far as I was concerned it was good riddance to the place.'

'Did you go on seeing Larry afterwards, Mandy?' Dorothea asked.

'Of course not. I had better things to do and better people to do them with. Anyway, as you know, I got into Art college, like I'd always wanted.' Mandy paused and looked searchingly at her friend, a glint of mischief in her eyes. 'I could ask you the same thing, Dottie?'

'What?'

'Did you go on seeing Larry when you went to work in the solicitors' firm where you met Charley?'

Dorothea was twisting the handle of her bag. For the moment she couldn't bring herself to answer. 'What do you mean, Mandy? Larry was your boyfriend.'

Mandy threw back her head, her laughter pealing out over the half-empty restaurant. 'Oh, Dottie, you're priceless! Did you think I didn't know? You with your ridiculous school-girl code. Of course I knew Larry was taking you out. He told me all about it. I didn't mind one bit. In fact I was really pleased. He was becoming the most awful bore—he'd no conversation beyond his job and who wants to listen to that when you've had it up to the teeth all day?'

Dorothea said nothing. She was glad to let Mandy keep on talking, the reminiscences softening her voice as she drew on images from the past.

'Poor Larry the Lamb... his idea of a night out was to take you to the pictures—he had two left feet when it came to dancing—and then slyly suggest you went back with him to the stock-room in the basement where he'd a cosy corner with carpet on the floorboards and an old blanket. A bit of a cuddle, he called it...' Mandy screwed up her face like a kitten about to sneeze. 'My God, all that dust, and rows of electric kettles beaming down at you! I said, no, thanks, I'd rather sleep in the park. He'd nowhere else to take a girl to. He had a real old harridan for a Mum, and he was saving up for a car. Did it never occur to you, Dorothea, that all those people at Higgs Electric used the place as if it were their home? It was pathetic...'

Dorothea took her up eagerly, anything to get away from the subject of Larry. 'You used to say Queenie'd been born under an office desk and brought herself up in a filing cabinet.'

'She was certainly built into the place—like those rats in the cellar. In fact, there was something very rat-like about our Queenie. That's what I said to Clive as we were driving back to London on the Sunday afternoon...'

Dorothea was horrified. 'You didn't tell this Clive person about seeing the Major with someone who looked like Queenie?'

'Why ever not? I couldn't keep such a sensational story to myself. It's the kind of thing I can dine out on for months—provided I can find out more... What are you looking at me like that for? It's more than just a bit of gossip. Of course it won't mean as much to other people as it does to you. Only you can really appreciate it, to them it'll only be a tale. They'll probably think I'm making it up.'

'Well, I'm still not sure that you're not.'

Mandy wasn't listening. A frown puckered the white skin of her forehead, and the laughter had gone out of her eyes.

'Dottie,' she said, 'you know what bothers me?'

'What, Mandy?'

'If it wasn't Queenie's body they found after the fire, then whose body was it?'

FOUR

IT HAD NOT BEEN EASY for Lennox Kemp to find a free evening to have his talk with Charles Copeland, and Charles too had difficulties. His wife had not been well, his son was about to sit an important examination for which Charles was coaching him. It was not until over a week later that Kemp and he were able to leave the office at six o'clock, stroll round the square to the Grapes and seek a quiet corner away from the drinkers at the bar.

'Everything all right at home?' Kemp inquired, setting down two half-pints. Charles did not reply immediately. He was folding his raincoat neatly to place it on a chair beside him. Nor would he have, even if not engaged on this small task. Charles had been impetuous in his youth, being a bright lad and at that time heedless of hurdles in his path. But long years in a careful profession, and he in situations which gave little scope for originality, had taught him to give guarded answers to the most innocuous of questions.

Now, as he arranged his coat satisfactorily and pushed himself into the bench, a wry recollection came unbidden to his mind.

As a junior clerk, standing waiting for instructions from Mr Archie Gillorn, the senior partner, Charles had anticipated the query his fellow-conspirators behind the half-closed door had told him would surely come. 'He'll ask you how are things at home. They often do when they haven't seen you before and can't remember who you are anyway... It's supposed to show they take an interest in the staff, but of course they never actually listen to what you say. Go on, Charley,' they'd urged, 'you try it ...'

In fact what Mr Archibald had said—for he was an astute old bird and did know something of Charles's circumstances—was: 'I hope your Father is keeping well, young man?' at the same time giving all his attention to the document he was signing.

'He's been taken to the Tower, sir, charged with high treason,' Charles had murmured, just loud enough to be heard beyond the door.

'Good. Good,' Mr Archibald had said, not raising his eyes. 'I'm glad to hear it. Now take this to the Bank immediately.'

Charles had received congratulations from his giggling mates, but he had an uneasy suspicion that the trick had been tried before.

He could not think why he should recall the occasion now, as he replied cautiously: 'Everything's fine at home, thank you, Mr Kemp.'

'You must be very proud of Ian. He did so well at school, and now I hear he's doing a course in accountancy.'

'Ian's all right,' said Charles; he was not one to boast of his son's success though secretly he was as pleased as his somewhat grudging nature would allow. 'My learning's a bit out of date, and I'm finding it difficult to catch up on computers, but I do my best to help the boy. Figures don't change, do they? Two and two still make four, eh?' He gave his dry laugh.

'Speaking of figures—' Kemp had not thought to get to the nub so early in the conversation but the casual juxtaposition of the words was a fair enough lead-in—'I see conveyancing is badly down in the monthly costs.'

Kemp was sorry to have to bring it up. Copeland didn't look well, and the lines on his face were deeper than they should have been in a man still in his early forties. The outward signs of scholarship might suit the features of an Oxford don, and aesthetically fit a Fellow of All Souls; on poor Charles Copeland they marked him simply as old before his time. The years of working by day and studying by night had taken their toll. Kemp wondered if there had been much enjoyment for Charley in the getting of knowledge, learning those inconsequential oddities, the feudal system of land tenures, the archaic writs of assumpsit, the evanescent principles of equity. Such historical drolleries Charley must have wrestled with in order to gain his eventual position.

Well, now he had to wrestle with more practical problems, competing in the market with entrepreneurs who wouldn't recognize a flying freehold if it smacked them in the eye; men who had no need to look beyond the value of property, its mortgage potential, and their clients' overweening desires.

Some of this emerged in their conversation now as Kemp skilfully drew the other man out.

'I can feel business slipping away from me,' said Charles, 'but I've no way to bring more in, I seem to have lost my grip on my clients ... And there's another man opened up in the Square. Jack Greggan. Used to be a clerk with Morgan, Smith until they fired him. Now he advertises in the local press. You know the kind of thing, Mr Kemp: Sell your house for a song, purchase at a premium. Some of our own clients who've been shopping around as they're advised to do these days, say he's cheap. I don't hold with undercutting, Mr Kemp.'

'Neither do I, Charles. And we shouldn't need to. We've managed to co-exist with these fellows these last few years.' He changed the subject abruptly. 'What's this about you not getting on with Mr Stoddart?'

Charles respected Kemp. Of all his employers so far he would grudgingly allow that Lennox Kemp was the best he had known. Kemp was fair, slow to blame, and was thoroughly conversant even with the details of routine work, for which he gave credit when it was due. To Charles, Kemp did seem to at least try to bridge the gulf between 'them' and 'us'.

'Mr Stoddart doesn't like me,' Charles answered slowly. 'I try not to let it bother me, but it's difficult in the branch office. At Clements Inn we ended up in different spheres and latterly I didn't see much of him . . .'

'What was the trouble there?'

'It's not for me to say, Mr Kemp. It was a long time ago . . .'

'But it worries you, this dislike?' Kemp spoke gently.

'I'll not deny that.' Charles took a gulp at his beer. 'Since he came I've not felt like doing my job as I should. I feel he's at my back all the time, finding fault. And there was that business of Brown Brothers.'

'Tell me.'

'Three years now I've done all their conveyancing. Like most builders, they like to keep to the same firm. Sales of land, building contracts, leasing of flats, selling their houses—they've always seemed satisfied. Then this last lot they're putting up on the Elgin estate, they've taken their business elsewhere—Morgan, Smith I think. I just can't understand it. I saw Peter Begg in the office the other day— he was settling a workmen's compensation case with Mr Stoddart—and he would hardly look me in the face. I've known Peter for years now, and we've always got on well.'

'So we're still doing their litigation?'

'Oh, that side's all right. It's the conveyancing we've lost, and that's meant a real blow to the costs taken in my department.'

Kemp considered what he'd been told by Elvira. There were undercurrents here which worried him, but already he sensed that Charles was becoming ill at ease. Grumbling to his superiors went against the grain of the man, and he must have been conscious of the complaining tone that had risen in his voice.

'I must be getting home.' Charles had looked at his watch. 'Otherwise Dorothea will be wondering where I've got to. She hasn't been well lately.'

'Why didn't you say so, Charles?'

'Didn't think you'd be interested, Mr Kemp.' Charles allowed himself the ghost of a smile. He looked better now than when he'd sat down, and it was not because of the beer. 'It's done me good having this chat, got it off my chest a bit. Sometimes you begin to think you're out on your own, that nobody really cares.'

'That's nonsense. Someone always cares. Now, what's this about Dorothea?' Kemp had met Charles's wife, a quiet, self-contained woman, he thought, devoted to her hard-working husband.

'She does suffer from migraine, but that's controlled by stuff she gets from her doctor. Unfortunately she's just had a bit of a shock. Something happened which upset her dreadfully...'

'What was it?'

'The death of an old friend—a woman friend. What's so awful about it was that Dot only read it in the paper a few days ago. Really knocked her, it did.'

'Was she a close friend?'

'They'd known each other for years. In fact, Dorothea had seen her only a week or so ago. Then there was this report in the Newtown paper about a body being found in the river, and it had been identified. You see, it was suicide, Mr Kemp.'

'You'd better get back to Dorothea, Charles. You should have told me sooner. Look, I'll walk you home. The air will do me good.'

The Copelands lived in a tree-lined road not far from the centre of the town. The neat houses with secluded gardens were older and larger than those on the new estates. Charles was a careful man and he earned a good salary; it was natural, being in the line he was, that he should invest in solid bricks and mortar.

The two men stopped at the wrought-iron gate, and Kemp was about to wish Charles goodnight when a light was switched on in the porch, the front door opened and a young man came running down the path.

'Oh, it's you, Dad. We saw you from the window and thought it was the police...'

'What do you mean, the police?'

'They phoned, Dad. About ten minutes ago. Said someone would be calling. It's about Mrs Egerton. I'm afraid it's upset Mum...'

'The police coming here? Oh Lord, whatever next!' Charles was already hurrying up the path to the door.

Kemp hesitated. Ian Copeland turned to him impulsively. 'I say, sir— It's Mr Kemp, isn't it? Would you mind coming in? It might help Mum and dad, you being there. The police said it was only routine, but...'

'Of course I'll come in if you want me to. Tell me, first, what exactly was the message from the police station?'

'Only that they'd found Mum was a friend of the dead woman, and had seen her recently. They said it was usual in the circumstances to contact anyone...well, anyone who...' the young man was floundering, obviously concerned for his mother.

Kemp asked no more questions, but followed Ian into the house.

Charles was on the sofa in the sitting-room with his arm round his wife's shoulders. Dorothea looked pale and red-eyed, as if she had been crying.

Kemp went over to them. 'Good evening, Mrs Copeland. I'm sorry I've kept Charles for so long, and do forgive me barging in like this but perhaps I can help. I know your friend's death must distress you, but it's perfectly normal for the police to make these inquiries. It may seem a bad moment to come but, believe me, they've no choice.'

Charles looked at him gratefully. 'I'm glad you're here, Mr Kemp. Dorothea and me, well, we've never had anything to do with the police before. That's more in your line.'

'I'll go and make you some tea, Mum, then you'll feel better.' Ian seemed a sensible young man.

Dorothea gave a wan smile, though it didn't reach her eyes.

'Everyone thinks women need tea at times of stress,' she said, 'though, oddly enough, it does help. Do sit down, Mr Kemp. And Charley, do stop fussing. I'm really all right now. It's just that things are happening so fast . . .'

Kemp took the chair opposite Dorothea.

'Tell me about your friend—this Mrs Egerton.'

'Mandy. I never think of her as anything else. She was Amanda Richards when I knew her first. That's over twenty years ago. We started work together, Mandy and I . . .'

'What did you see about her in the paper?'

She tightened pale lips, but straightened her back as if determined to at least keep that under control.

'It was a small item in the *Newtown Gazette*. Was it last Saturday's, Charley?'

He nodded.

'I couldn't believe it,' Dorothea went on in her level, rather colourless voice. 'It said the body of a woman taken from the River Lea had been identified as . . . Amanda Egerton of Northside Avenue in Enfield. That was Mandy's address . . .'

'And you'd seen her recently?'

'When would it be, Charley? The week before last. A Tuesday. Yes, that was it. My usual day at the Save the Children shop . . .'

'Did you and Mrs Egerton often meet?'

Dorothea frowned, brown blotches standing out from the pallor of her skin. She twisted her fingers in her lap. Before she could answer, the doorbell pealed. 'I'll get it.' Charles jumped to his feet.

If Detective-Sergeant Cobbins was uncomfortable he did not show it. He had a soothing way with him, and the ability to put the nervous at their ease. Kemp had seen him do it many times, breaking bad news, calming reluctant or hysterical witnesses. It may have been because Cobbins had been a countryman before joining the force, and he had the countryman's instinct to take things slowly, and to be patient.

He had had the sense not to be in uniform, and he sat now accepting a cup of tea as though he were simply a friendly caller. He explained that in the course of inquiries into the background of the dead woman they had come upon the name of Dorothea Copeland.

'It was in her diary which she kept at her business address. She was going to have lunch with you on—' he glanced, briefly, at his notebook—'Tuesday, January 12th. Did she keep that appointment with you, Mrs Copeland?'

Dorothea nodded.

'And her secretary—a Miss Rachel Freeman—told us she often spoke about you. It seems Mrs Egerton told her you were her oldest friend—' he coughed—'oldest and dearest were the words used, I understand.'

Tears gathered in Dorothea's eyes, blurring their dark blue.

'Were you able to obtain any relevant information concerning Mrs Egerton's state of mind from the people she worked with, Sergeant?' Kemp asked, to give Dorothea time to recover.

'We weren't, Mr Kemp. Apparently she seemed quite normal in behaviour at her place of business in Kensington, though they didn't see that much of her. She travelled a lot. In the fashion trade, I believe. They spoke highly of her, and she appears to have been popular. No money worries, either. According to her bank, she was nicely placed, financially speaking. That's why we've come to you, Mrs Copeland, you being so close to her . . .'

'Oh, but I wasn't!' Dorothea burst out, then, feeling their eyes upon her, she stopped.

'When you had lunch with her that day, did your friend seem to be depressed about anything?'

'Just the opposite,' Dorothea exclaimed, seeing Mandy's face in front of her, laughing. 'She was excited...but then she always was...very vivacious. I've never known her to be depressed.'

'What did you talk about? I mean, did she give any indication that there was something on her mind? Was she worried about anything?'

'Mandy had no worries. She always had plenty of money, and she loved to spend it. She was mad about clothes, and was forever buying something...' As if she was afraid her words were giving the wrong impression, she added: 'Of course that was her career—fashion, so one couldn't blame her.'

'What about health? Could she have been anxious about her health?'

'Mandy? She never had so much as a headache in her whole life!' Dorothea pressed her fingers to her own forehead. Charles watched with growing concern. 'My wife gets bad migraines... Don't you think she's answered enough questions, Sergeant?'

Mr Cobbins got to his feet, put his notebook in his pocket.

'I'm sorry I've had to upset her. There was just the off-chance that Mrs Copeland might have some ideas why her friend should take her own life, and it's always better if we can get these inquiries over before the inquest.'

'When will that be, Mr Cobbins?' Kemp asked.

'Thursday. There'll be no need for Mrs Copeland to attend—unless that is she would want to—'

Dorothea shook her head, her eyes already half-closed as she fought off the first symptoms of approaching pain.

'I don't want to go,' she whispered, 'I've never been in a court...'

'I'll go, if you like, Dorothea,' Kemp said to her, then he turned to Charles. 'Don't come to the office tomorrow, Charles, you stay with your wife. I think she will need you.'

'I'll see how she is tomorrow, and get her doctor. But thanks, anyway.' He went back to his wife and put his arm round her.

Ian showed Kemp and Sergeant Cobbins out. The Sergeant's car was at the gate. 'Looks like I'll get a lift home,' said Kemp cheerfully. 'Your mother will be all right, Ian, I think the worst of the shock is over.'

As they drove off Sergeant Cobbins spoke in the ruminative tone people tend to adopt when voicing a universal truth: 'Rotten business, suicide...always leaves a nasty taste.'

'H'm...I suppose they're sure it was suicide?'

'Oh yes. She left a note.'

'You didn't say...'

'Not my job to, Mr Kemp. It'll keep for the inquest.'

'Was it addressed to anyone?'

'I don't think so, certainly not to Mrs Copeland or they'd have informed me. Apparently it took the form of a letter found in the dead lady's car. And it was that abandoned car, a brand new Escort automatic, that drew the matter to our attention in the first place. A workman noticed it for a couple of mornings when he was crossing a disused road down by the old gravel pits, and he thought he'd better report it. One of our constables had a look, and in view of what was found in the car, the area was searched. The body was found in the river under the reeds.'

'Could it have been an accident?'

'No chance. That car was on firm ground. It was unlocked. Her handbag was in it, driver's licence, credit cards—the lot. And I gather this note she left was there too. Looks like she drove to the spot herself deliberately. Lonely place, no one around, ideal if you've mind to suicide, and it seems she had. Only her fingerprints on the steering-wheel. They're giving the car a good going-over, of course. It was the Met at Enfield went to her home, and got a positive identification from folks there. That led to finding her diary, and me visiting Mrs Copeland because of that entry.'

'How far from the car to the river?'

'A good few yards from the edge. They reckon she just got out, walked over to the bank and threw herself in.'

Kemp considered the January weather. 'Must have been cold.'

'Too bloody cold. She wouldn't have lasted long... Here we are, then, Mr Kemp, right at your door.'

'Thanks, Mr Cobbins.' Kemp thought for a moment before he got out. 'Would you buy a new car if you were contemplating suicide?'

The Sergeant shrugged. 'There's no telling. The more I learn about people, Mr Kemp, the less I know.'

FIVE

CHARLES COPELAND telephoned Kemp the next morning. Dorothea had had an uneasy night, and the doctor would be calling to see her before midday. Charles was about to insist he come into the office in the afternoon, but Kemp cut him off and ordered him to stay at home.

'I've already had a word with Mr Lambert, and he assures me there's nothing urgent that he can't deal with,' he told Charles, 'and a day off won't do you any harm, Charles.'

It'll give me the opportunity to tackle Nick Stoddart, he thought, while Charley's out of the way.

First, Kemp had plenty of his own clients to see, and there was that difficult letter to draft for the soothing of souls at Head Office. He assured them that a temporary drop in conveyancing costs wasn't the end of civilization as they knew it, and that springtime, that pretty ringtime, would soon be here with nesting birds and wedding bells to gladden their hearts with an upsurge in the figures. Elvira cut out the lyrical bits.

Mr Stoddart was in the County Court for most of the day, indulging his penchant for fancy legal argument in some rather shoddy little landlord and tenant cases, so that it was not until late in the afternoon that he allowed he could spare an hour for discussion with Mr Kemp.

The two men scarcely knew one another, and were therefore wary without outward hostility during the first few minutes' chat on matters affecting the branch office, clients they had in common, and the state of litigation in general. Stoddart did most of the talking. He was broad of shoulder and small in the head, giving the impression of a cardboard cut-out, but seemed unaware of the peculiarity, having a great conceit of himself which was manifest in the somewhat smug complacency of his undeniably handsome features. He'd look fine in a barrister's wig, thought Kemp, it would have a balancing effect. Had he ever considered it? Not surprisingly, Nick Stoddart had.

'I'd like to have read for the Bar,' he confided. 'I knew I had the brains for it, but it took money and the going was too slow for me.'

So, he thinks he's squandering those cerebral assets on the lowlier side of the profession, reflected Kemp, amused.

'You were articled to Mr Archibald Gillorn, weren't you, Nick?'

'Yes, and did the obligatory assistant stint with them, but afterwards I got a better offer from Becketts in the City, and went there for a few years. Unfortunately their ideas on promotion didn't match mine. When I heard Gillorns had a gap in their litigation department I went back to them, and by Jove, they were glad to have me! Litigation's my forte...'

'So I understand.' Kemp was getting rather tired of the man's presumption; small the head might look but if it swelled up any further it would burst. 'You must have known Charles Copeland a long time?'

'Well, hardly known him. Charley was more or less an office boy when I started at Gillorns. I suppose he thought because I was the articled clerk he was in the same position as me. He never seemed to recognize the difference. He was a proper little prig in those days.'

'Was he? That doesn't sound like our Charley.'

'Always thought he was in the right. Too clever by half. It's no secret that we didn't get on. But of course, we went our separate ways—that was bound to happen. It's only now our paths have crossed again.'

'You say you didn't get on. Any particular reason?'

'Just that he was a slimy little bastard. I don't mince my words, Lennox.'

'I've noticed. What was the trouble between you?'

Nick Stoddart brought out cigarettes, and both men lit up, Kemp watching the other man carefully.

'It was a long time ago,' said Nick finally. 'I don't want to be the one to rake up old sores...'

'It's bad in a small office like ours that you hold a grudge against Charles, and that you show it.'

'He's a creep, and I don't care who knows it. I simply can't understand how you came to give him charge of a department.'

'If you know any cogent reason why I shouldn't, I'd be glad if you'll tell me.'

'I'm not one to tell tales out of school.' The expression convinced Kemp that Stoddart would, and take pleasure in the exercise.

Kemp made a sudden movement of impatience, toppling the neat pile of documents placed by Elvira on one side of his desk. As he retrieved them, and stuck them firmly under a paperweight, he was conscious of a growing distaste for the interview, despite having been the one to initiate it. 'I don't want to hear it, Nick,' he said, levelly, 'if as you say it's all in the past.'

But Stoddart now had the bit between his teeth and, being the man he was, there was no stopping him.

'When I got here and found that Charley'd wormed his way in, I couldn't credit it...a jumped-up, snivelling clerk like him!'

'I don't think this conversation should go any further.'

'You started it. Oh, Charley's been clever all right, getting into your good books. Quite the little sea-green incorruptible he is in this office.' The sneer came easily, and sat well on the full, sensuous mouth; it must have struck terror into many a nervous miscreant.

Kemp tapped a pencil on the desk, curbing anger. Really, Stoddart was a difficult character to deal with. Hard to tell whether his manner was simply an extension of his normal courtroom style or whether it showed he had a genuine grievance against Copeland. Kemp's curiosity overcame his finer feelings.

'Come on then, Nick, out with it. What was the trouble between you and Charles?'

But under cross-examination you never answer directly if you want to lead your questioner by the nose into deeper waters, so Stoddart hedged. 'Just giving you a hint, old boy... I'm not the one to stir up faction...' Catching Kemp's blankly disbelieving stare, he modified his tone. 'All I'm saying is, don't take Charley Copeland at his face value just because he's been twenty years working his way up.'

Kemp recognized the attempt to fudge the issue, the tactic of the hidden slander, the smear too nebulous to be refuted, too damaging to ignore. 'What do you mean,' he inquired lightly, 'by face value? Charley's not a bit of antique silver.'

Stoddart liked the metaphor. He gave a short laugh. 'If he was, he'd be found to weigh less than sterling, I can tell you.'

'Then why don't you?'

When he put his mind to it, Kemp could be as artful as anybody in extracting information. He did it by stubborn persistence, and by reiteration of the very question he deemed the other person was unwilling to answer. So now he said again: 'What was the trouble between you?'

'I think I've said enough...'

'You've said nothing.'

'Well,' Stoddart drawled, 'I simply didn't want you taken in by him. All this conscientious loyal servant of the firm act Charley puts on...it's sickening.'

'Go on.' Kemp continued to stare at the lawyer with blank opaque grey eyes as if contemplating an insect on a leaf. The cool indifference behind that look made it the more intimidating.

'Oh, all right then. You asked for it...' Nick Stoddart felt he'd made enough virtuous protestations. 'Years ago I caught Charley taking a bribe, accepting money from a client in return for a favour.' He stopped, but observing no visible reaction in Kemp's unwavering look, he continued.

'I was the only one in the firm who knew about it. He'd covered himself pretty well, thought he was being clever, no doubt. But I knew...'

'And?'

'Well, of course I tackled him...and in the end he had to admit to having taken money.'

'How much, and what for?'

'After all this time I can't remember the details. Water under the bridge by now... Anyway, by the time I found out it was too late to do anything—the case was over and done with. The amount was petty enough, though I'll bet it wasn't to Charley. Five hundred pounds.'

Kemp wondered why Stoddart who couldn't or wouldn't recall the circumstances seemed to have no difficulty in remembering the amount involved.

'Did you report what you'd found to the senior members of the firm?'

Stoddart gave another of his short, barking laughs. 'No, I didn't. I was younger then and a damned sight more soft-hearted than I am now. I was sorry for the blighter, I suppose... He gave me some sob-story about wanting to get married, and not having enough for the down payment on the house...'

'And you fell for it?' There was more than a hint of mockery now in Kemp's eyes.

'You have to understand, Lennox, Charley and I at that time were knocking about together. I don't say we were bosom friends but he tended to look upon me as one of his mates. Of course he never really cottoned on to the difference between us—that we'd not stay the way we were. He pleaded with me not to tell. So I didn't. No one had been harmed by his taking the money...'

'What was the case about?'

'I've told you, I can't possibly remember after this length of time. He did this client a favour, and the client made him a payment on the side. It's not unknown.'

'Isn't it? I should have thought it was, in a reputable outfit like Gillorns.'

'But that's just the point,' Stoddart said eagerly. 'If I'd told them, Charley would have been sacked on the spot. He'd have been out on his ear without a reference to his name!'

'Why are you telling me this now?'

'Because you asked me.' Stoddart sounded peeved; perhaps he hadn't got quite the response from Kemp that he'd hoped for. 'And because I think you ought to know that Charley Copeland isn't the model of probity everyone seems to think...'

'What do you want me to do about it, Nick? Fire him? For something you say he did—what?—twenty years ago.'

Stoddart didn't answer. He shifted uncomfortably in his seat as if unsure whether he should get up and go, or wait to be dismissed which would hurt his dignity. His handsome features had taken on a look of petulance. He's a bad loser in Court, thought Kemp dispassionately, the kind who bundles his files away in a thumping great temper and blames his own witnesses, his client or the Judge—never himself. He'd had enough of Stoddart.

On the other hand there was something more here than a long-held grievance.

'You and Charley, starting in the firm about the same time, you'd be friends at first... You were friends, weren't you?' he inquired mildly, interested that Stoddart's eyes should flicker at the word.

'He would say that we'd been friends. It would be to his advantage. But, believe you me, Lennox, as soon as I found out what he'd been up to... well, I distanced myself from him pretty fast.' Self-righteousness was a mantle which fitted smoothly on Stoddart's shoulders.

With his own early experience as a background, Kemp could see clearly how it might have been: the two young men in that office in Clements Inn, thrown together at the outset of their careers, each eager to make his way.

They would both have had to study, but in their off-duty times they would have, as Nick put it, 'knocked around together'. Two clerks in the legal world, learning their trade in the Courts, exploring the corridors and the cubby-holes of the Registries, running errands for the firm—and putting on airs in the drinking places at lunch-time round Chancery Lane. Each would be determined to get on.

Yes, they could well have been friends, their relationship closer perhaps than Stoddart, with his airy assumption of superiority, would now admit. Above them soared the hierarchy of the profession, a mountain to be climbed from that base camp, although only one was destined for the summit. That might have been a situation in which seeds of resentment could have been sown, but if so, then it would surely have been on Charles's side...

Kemp was conscious that Nick was waiting for him to speak.

'All right, Nick,' he said flatly, 'you've told me. But whatever this indiscretion of Charles's was—and for the moment I'll call it no more than that—it's in the past. I want no talk of it here in this office. Do I make myself plain?'

The other man got to his feet. His thickset body had presence, his thrusting shoulders set to overawe lesser mortals. Faced with someone not impressed, his qualities dwindled, and now he shuffled his fine leather brogues uncertainly on Kemp's strip of carpet.

'Just thought you ought to know,' he grumbled. 'You can't expect me to carry on working in the same place as Charley Copeland and totally ignore what I think of him.'

'Not if you make it obvious,' said Kemp coldly. 'I want you to understand here and now that I won't put up with any denigration of either him or his work so long as I'm in charge here.'

Stoddart wagged his chunky little head up and down several times like a drinking duck before he smiled, not with any amusement, and when the smile got as far as his eyes it turned very nasty indeed. 'Of course, I should have realized,' he said, 'you and Charley are birds of a feather. You've both committed what you'd call indiscretions in the past. You got found out and were struck off...Charley was luckier. But, yes, I can appreciate your sympathy for him. You've had your hands in the till yourself.'

Allusions to Kemp's own fall from grace in the profession were rarely made to him these days; he had paid his debt, and his integrity was no longer in doubt. So far as he himself was concerned, he had learned to ride out the occasional snipe from the disaffected. His record was no secret, nor had it ever been, so that Stoddart's remark merely deepened his dislike of the man and called for no comment. He kept up his steady gaze at the other lawyer but did nothing to hide the contempt in his eyes. Disconcerted, Stoddart turned on his heel. He closed the door behind him with a bang. Kemp winced at the sound, and sighed. It wasn't going to be easy to restore peace within this small domain of his. He would have to speak to Charles again, though he had no heart for the task. Stoddart had been careful, he knew enough to avoid outright slander, his method was the sly insinuation, a hint here, a nudge there... Kemp knew sufficient of his profession to recognize the danger, and reluctant as he was to have to bring the matter up with Charles Copeland again, it would have to be done.

It was never wise to leave a stain untreated, it would soon become ingrained and withstand all washing. Good house-wifely advice, he thought ruefully, and as such he would have to follow it, no matter how distasteful.

SIX

THE INQUEST on Mrs Amanda Egerton was held in a small dark room behind the Newtown Magistrates' Court. Apart from the Court functionaries there were a few present, and Lennox Kemp slid unobtrusively into a seat at the rear. He knew the District Coroner slightly. Mr Everard Harvey was an experienced lawyer, not given to wasting his own or other people's time by making the kind of controversial remarks that lent colour, and publicity, to the courts of some of his fellow coroners. Mr Harvey was there to perform an official duty, he knew precisely what that duty was and he would carry it through in the minimum of time necessary.

Evidence was given by the police as to their search of the car reported abandoned beside the old gravel pit called Pender's Pond. An envelope containing the letter found on the dashboard of the car was handed to the Coroner, who opened it, briefly perused the contents and placed it on the table in front of him without comment. The evidence continued with the subsequent search of the river itself, and the discovery of the body of a woman.

Identification of the deceased was made by a Mr Albert Collins who was evidently much moved. Under Mr Harvey's kindly direction, however, he recovered and gave his evidence clearly. He said that his wife, Clara Collins, was cook-housekeeper to Mrs Egerton at No. 10 Northside Avenue, Enfield, and he also lived there as handyman and gardener. They had been in their respective employments at that address for some fifteen years, initially with Mrs Egerton's mother, and on her death had remained in the service of her daughter. They were both very fond of Mrs Egerton, and deeply distressed by hearing from the police that she had died. Mr Collins had accompanied the police to the morgue, and his identification of the body was positive.

She had been last seen by them on the morning of Tuesday, January 19th, when she had told Mrs Collins not to prepare dinner that night as she would possibly be away. No, they had not been worried by her absence; Mrs Egerton travelled a lot and was often away on business for two or three days at a time. She always carried an overnight case in her car for this purpose, and the one found in the back seat of the Escort was hers, the clothing having been identified by Mrs Collins, and the car itself belonged to the deceased, Mr Collins having been responsible for its cleaning and maintenance. Neither he nor his wife could give any reason why Mrs Egerton should take her own life; she was a happy woman, he said, a good employer. Speaking of her, Mr Collins was again overcome, and he was thanked and allowed to be seated.

The next witness, Mr Sydney Silbert, was a thin, intense individual with dark, upswept hair and a sallow skin. He was the director of the design company for whom Mrs Egerton worked from time to time. He explained that she had been a freelance designer who sold much of her work abroad and in the Midlands but when in London she used their Kensington offices as a base. Amanda, he said, had been at her desk most of the previous week working hard on some new designs. She had been her normal self, and he described her as a bright, very competent woman with a real flair for fashion, and considerable artistic skills. Answering more searching questions, he said she was popular with others in the trade... 'She was always so full of life, she had a vibrant personality which affected all who knew her...' No, neither he nor any of his colleagues in the office had seen any change in her recently. She had been perhaps more excited than usual the last time he'd talked to her, which was just before lunch on the 19th, and he thought it was the prospect of her going over to the Paris collections. 'But she was always high-spirited,' he added, 'there was always an air of excitement about Amanda...' No, he'd never seen her depressed. She took her work seriously but it never worried her. So far as he knew, she had no financial anxieties. On the contrary, he understood her to have private means, but in any case she was in a position to put a high price on her sketches alone.

Financial matters were dealt with briefly by Mrs Egerton's lawyer, Mr Brunt, an elderly, soft-spoken man who said he'd been her family's solicitor for many years. Mrs Egerton was an only child who had inherited the house in Enfield from her mother along with very adequate capital. She had been married twice, both times to men of some wealth; there had been two quiet, amicable divorces, 'with,' he said drily, 'satisfactory settlements in each case.'

There were no children of either marriage. The first husband had since died, the second remarried and was living in Australia. There were no other relatives. Mr Brunt had not seen Mrs Egerton since the last divorce, when he had advised her to make a new will. Yes, the will had been drawn up at that time and duly executed. He would not divulge the contents since they had no bearings on the present proceedings. As one lawyer to another, Mr Harvey did not press him on the point, being more concerned, as was his duty, to establish simply the cause of death and, in the circumstances, the state of mind of the deceased immediately prior to her demise. Mr Brunt made it clear that she had had no financial worries.

Kemp guessed from the tone of Mr Brunt's evidence that he had not altogether approved of Mrs Egerton's way of life. 'She lived extravagantly,' he lisped, 'but she had adequate means to do so...'

The Coroner handed him the letter found in the car, and asked him if it was in Mrs Egerton's writing. 'There is no need to read it closely,' he said, 'the meaning is clear.' He had said the same thing to Mr Collins and to Sydney Silbert. They all acknowledged that the handwriting was indeed that of Mrs Egerton.

Kemp had been listening to the various witnesses without taking notes beyond their names and addresses, which he thought might be useful should Dorothea Copeland wish to get in touch with any of them later. He did, however, lend a more careful ear when the body itself was being discussed with true medical dispassion by Dr Albury, the pathologist, since he and Albury had met before on other cases of sudden death in the district.

The pathologist had read his report stolidly, giving the brute facts which led inevitably to his conclusion that the death of Mrs Egerton was due to drowning, air having been prevented from entering the air-passages and lungs by the water in which the body was found, and the signs of asphyxia had been present on the post-mortem examination.

The pathologist had been one of the first to be called, his evidence being vital to establishing cause of death—and Mr Harvey being well aware that doctors are always in a hurry, rushing about in pursuit of bugs, drugs and vagrant viruses. Albury had been excused early in the proceedings so that he could return to whatever urgent hospital duties required his expertise.

It was therefore with some surprise that Kemp became aware that the doctor had slipped into a seat not far from himself, and was listening intently to the other evidence.

Such evidence having now been completed, the Coroner took up the letter from his table, adjusted his spectacles and read it through twice. He replaced it, clasped his hands in front of him, and quietly addressed the small gathering. In a few succinct words he covered the information gained from the various witnesses; made the point that the police had found no signs of struggle, only one set of footprints from the car to the river, hers, that foul play could probably be ruled out, and accident did not appear feasible . . .

He had paused there, and added, 'unfortunately'. A kind man, he would have preferred, 'death by misadventure'. He dwelt delicately on the few facts elicited on Mrs Egerton's personal life from which nothing had emerged to show it had recently become unhappy; discreet inquiries had shown she had had no strong attachment to any person immediately prior to her death.

Kemp could feel that Mr Harvey was steadily approaching the inevitable verdict. He would be pleased there would be no need for the usual consoling words to the bereaved, no sorrowing relatives to be absolved from blame; it would matter to no one that he had no other course but to find that Amanda Egerton had taken her own life.

Mr Harvey was still speaking when there was a hurried movement close to where Kemp was sitting, and footsteps sounded down the center aisle between the empty chairs. He realized that Dr Albury was in the front of the room. The Coroner paused, and raised his eyebrows.

'Yes, Dr Albury?'

'I'm sorry, sir... There was something perhaps I should have added in my report.'

Mr Harvey frowned. 'I assume it is relevant? Very well, please return to the stand.'

'I didn't mention it before because it was no part of the cause of death. In fact, I wouldn't report it now except that I've listened to what the witnesses have said about the—er—deceased, and that she didn't seem to have any reason to commit suicide...' Doctors tend to use the proper words. 'I'd expected to hear that there might be one of the usual reasons, financial circumstances, trouble at work, or a broken love-affair—but it seems she was a happy woman until...' he hesitated.

'Say what you have to say, Doctor.'

Separated from his brief, Albury was not so word-perfect; he sought the aid of his report.

'On examination of the body I found there was a small tumour in the left breast. Not a large growth, you understand, but one that had been palpable.'

'Would the deceased have been aware of it?'

'I can't truthfully answer that. As I say, it was palpable. It would depend on whether she was the kind of woman to be aware of any change in her breast tissue...'

'Are you saying Mrs Egerton had a cancerous growth?'

'In the circumstances, sir, and bearing in mind the state of the body, no one could tell whether or not the tumour was malignant. All I'm saying is that it was a lump that could have been felt, particularly by a woman whose body was otherwise healthy and well cared for.'

The Coroner pursed his lips. He again picked up the letter and read it through once more. He nodded, as if satisfied.

'Thank you for bringing this to our attention, Doctor. We are obliged to you.'

Albury retreated to his seat in silence which was broken by an exclamation from Sydney Silbert: 'Oh my God...poor Amanda!'

A sharp glance from Mr Harvey stilled any further interruption, as he said: 'I do not think it necessary for me to make public what is in this letter, but in the further light Dr Albury has shed on this unhappy occurrence I can now say there is clear indication that Mrs Egerton did contemplate taking her own life...'

Everard Harvey would be well satisfied, thought Kemp wryly, he was presented with the *actus reus*, all he was waiting for was the *mens rea*, and the Doctor seemed to have provided it...

After the verdict had been delivered in the Coroner's quiet, precise tone, there was a moment's uneasy silence as if people were saying to themselves, 'Is that it, then?' before they pushed back their chairs and filtered out into the bright winter sunshine.

Kemp caught Dr Albury as the latter was getting into his car.

'Hullo, Lennox. What are you doing here? Did you know the dead woman?'

Kemp shook his head. 'I'm here on behalf of a friend. Tell me, if Mrs Egerton had known she had a lump in her breast, what would be the first thing she'd do?'

Albury sighed. 'I don't know. Women all react differently. Most would rush off and tell their nearest and dearest. Some would go immediately to their GP. Others might think about it, brood over it, get depressed, and do nothing. Some would ignore it, hoping it would just go away. And, of course, in Mrs Egerton's case I can't be sure she even knew... It was very small, a very early manifestation.'

'And if she had gone to a GP, what would he have told her?'

'To have tests done,' said Albury, 'to find out whether it was benign or not. Of course tests wouldn't show up on the body, except that no biopsy had been carried out on this one... There's no way of telling now, Lennox, whether this woman knew what she had.'

'Thanks.'

Kemp watched the doctor drive off, then he returned to the building. He found Mr Brunt and Mr Harvey deep in conversation but they appeared to be discussing the date for the next meeting of the local Law Society; so far as they were concerned, their interest in the late Mrs Egerton had ceased. Mr Brunt, however, paused long enough to give Kemp the details of where and when the funeral would take place, and, on hearing that Kemp was there on behalf of Mrs Copeland he mentioned he would be getting in touch with her, as she would be receiving a small legacy from the deceased.

Kemp sauntered into the little office where the Clerk of the Court was gathering up the few papers into its thin file. Kemp had a word with him.

'You say you're acting on behalf of a close friend of the dead woman, Mr Kemp? Well, I see no harm in it. It's a sad letter...'

He gave it to Kemp, extracting it from the official envelope, in which it had been placed for its brief court appearance. It was only a short note, written in a sprawling but elegant hand on paper torn from a pad of good quality stationery, pale buff in colour. It looked as if the writer had used a ballpoint, for at the top of the letter the ink had not been flowing properly and there were mere indentations in the paper until the pen had been pressed to it more firmly.

Kemp copied the contents quickly into his notebook. He held the letter up to the light from the window for a moment, then returned it to the Clerk, and thanked him.

As he walked over to his car, Kemp thought that in many ways it made things easier, what he had to tell Mrs Copeland. It was surely no disgrace to fear one form of death, and hasten that end by other means... Would that console Dorothea for the loss of her friend, or would she be the more sorrowful because that friend had not confided in her? Never as much as a headache in her life, she'd said of Mandy... What was that long, twenty-year friendship worth if not to support one another in the crises of later life?

Friendship. Those bonds forged in adolescence, or in one's first job, in the early stages of careers... Kemp was suddenly reminded of another friendship just as old, Nick Stoddart and Charles Copeland. What price that friendship now?

At least Amanda Egerton had remembered her friend; Mr Brunt had indicated the legacy was small, he'd hinted at a couple of thousand, but everything is relative and Kemp thought Dorothea Copeland would consider it a fortune. Most of the estate, Mr Brunt had indicated, was to go to charitable purposes, and he had spoken approvingly; well, it was he who had drafted the will.

SEVEN

DOROTHEA HAD NOT BEEN happy to have Charles at home with her for two whole days. She should have been, and felt familiar guilt because she was not. She wanted desperately to be alone with her thoughts, but Charles had insisted on sitting with her, fussing and bringing meals to her as if she was an invalid. The doctor had been, prescribed stronger tablets for migraine should it recur, but the headaches had gone, her vision was no longer blurred, the sickness had passed, and she was left with a tremendous sense of well-being. She surmised the doctor would have said it was pure reaction, but that Dorothea doubted. She felt almost indecently healthy in body, and more alert in her mind than she had been in months. Of course she felt guilty about that, too. She should be grieving for Mandy, Mandy who had been so full of life and was now dead. But, as she had told Mr Kemp and the policeman, she and Mandy had not been close...

What would he have to say when he came from the inquest? Charley had asked him to have supper with them. 'It's the least we can do when he's taken that burden from our shoulders,' he'd said, and Dorothea was busying herself making a special meal, for she knew Mr Kemp lived alone and would appreciate it. She was a good cook, patient and meticulous, if lacking in originality, and now that the headaches had gone she put Charley firmly out of the kitchen and took control.

But as she chopped mint for the sauce, peeled potatoes and cut vegetables, pictures of Mandy came into her head with a clarity that startled her, as if she was seeing them through pale green water, transparent as glass. She stopped, her knife poised. As Mandy had reminded her, there were moments when Dorothea had the gift—or the bane—of total recall.

She saw the two desks, one on either side of the telephone cabinet—that awful contraption which neither she nor Mandy had ever got the hang of. She saw the whole of that seedy office, the blacked-out window high on the wall, the dusty grey filing cabinets, and the half-partition screening the Major's quarters at the far end. She saw Mandy as she'd seen her that first day; the short black mini-skirt, plump schoolgirl legs, a maroon sweater showing off the full bosom, and rising from the heavy roll-collar the pink-and-white perfection of her face. She remembered now what she had thought then: '...the small face buoyant, like a bell-flower on its bed... O'er the breast's superb abundance...'

Dorothea had been seventeen, just out of school, and half of her lingered there still in the safe fields of English literature.

She frowned, shook herself, and crossed to the oven to baste the roasting meat.

As she carried the spoon to the draining-board and it dropped with a clink on the stainless steel surface, Mandy appeared to her again. Instead of the neat garden beyond the kitchen window Dorothea was looking at the dingy ballroom, hung with tinsel for the company's event of the year, the annual dance and salesmen's booze-up, and there was Mandy in tight bronze-coloured satin whirling round in the arms of Larry the Lamb, her bubble-cut hair spiked with yellow making her look like a great curly chrysanthemum.

Dorothea shook herself, this time more briskly. Sheer nonsense, she scolded herself, it's only word-association; I'm cooking lamb so I think of Larry—and that's nonsense, too. I've not thought of him in years—not until

Mandy reminded me. And I don't want to think of that either...

For Charley's sake, she must keep calm, calm and pleasant in front of their guest. Dorothea had read about wives who tried to impress their husband's employers by corrupting them with kitchen comforts... Sceptical soul that she was, Dorothea would normally have disdained such effort but tonight it was important that Mr Kemp should receive the right impression. She had some doubts; from what she'd heard of him, he was not easy to impress...

DOROTHEA NEED NOT have worried; it was not of her that Lennox Kemp was thinking as he drove up to their house at seven o'clock that evening, but of her husband.

When one has become used to regarding a person in a certain light, worked with them for some time, and generally known them in even the minimal accepted sense, one attaches attributes to them which tend to stick and are not easily dislodged.

Kemp had put Charles like a snapshot into a corner of his mind; the pale, lined, young-old face, thinning brown hair, the sharp yet tired eyes, and the slightly stooped figure. A plodder, Kemp had thought, but an able one, diligent in his duties, careful to the point of nitpicking in his attention to detail. The picture had seemed to Kemp to be the man himself, but if he took that snapshot out now it would be smudged. No matter that he might read the character of Nick Stoddart as meretricious, and surprisingly vengeful after all these years, there still remained that blur on the image of Charles.

Some time, he would have to have a discreet word with him. But first, Dorothea.

Kemp scarcely knew her, since before this episode they had met only at semi-official functions. These were rare, Kemp taking the view that his fellow workers, from lawyers to cleaning staff, were sufficiently adult to form their own associations and friendships, in or out of the office, without benefit of frolics provided by the firm. He knew he was possibly alone in this opinion; some firms went out of their way to encourage jolly get-togethers to promote the corporate image—often with dire effect. The supply of free alcohol could lead to dishevelled high jinks, and occasionally the hitherto unspoken being voiced, with devastating results. Morale tended to be lower after such affairs—which was hardly their aim.

Had he been pressed to give his candid impression of Dorothea Copeland after such brief encounters as they'd had, he would have been forced to admit that he found her dull, stilted in conversation, and, apart from a dutiful approbation of her husband, lacking in any spark of interest or character.

However, if he'd been wrong in his assessment of Charles, he could easily have been wrong about her, too.

The evening was initially somewhat sticky. As Charles diffidently offered sherry, dry or medium sweet, it was obvious that the Copelands didn't usually have drinks before dinner—which in any case they called supper. However, the small ceremony of glasses on a tray gave Kemp the opportunity to give them the bald facts concerning the verdict at the inquest.

Apart from a drawing-in of her lips, and a glistening in her eyes when he spoke of Dr Albury's evidence, Dorothea seemed to have her feelings under control. As she kept going to and fro between the sitting-room and the kitchen, it was difficult for Kemp to determine what effect his words were having on her.

'But that's quite impossible,' she'd murmured when he'd reported that a tumour of some kind had been found. 'Mandy would have told me.'

'She may not have known,' said Kemp, elaborating on his subsequent conversation with the pathologist, 'or she only

found out during those last few days, and since she'd had
lunch with you.'

Dorothea had shaken her head decisively. 'She didn't
know that day. She couldn't have. She was in such high
spirits. She was excited . . .'

'Could that have been because she knew?'

'Not that sort of excitement!' Dorothea's eyes suddenly
flared, anger in them. 'How can you say such a thing!' She
rose hastily, putting her glass down on the small, round,
carefully-polished table so that the liquid splashed its surface. 'I must go and see to the roast.'

Over the meal, which by Kemp's admittedly low standard, used as he was to his own somewhat scratch culinary
efforts, was an admirable one, he gave them more details of
the inquest.

'I know about Mr Brunt,' Dorothea remarked, 'Mandy
used to imitate him—old Fuddy-Duddy she called him, but
I think she really liked him.'

'Did you ever meet either of the husbands?'

'Only the first. Bernard. He was nice. Of course he was a
lot older than Mandy. She was about twenty-four when she
married him. Remember, Charley, we went there to dinner? They had a flat in Hampstead.'

'It was a bit out of our class,' said Charles awkwardly.
'You said so yourself, Dot . . .'

'You see, Mr Kemp,' Dorothea explained earnestly,
'Mandy and I didn't see so much of each other once we were
both married. We moved in different circles. It changed
things . . . Of course she and I would still meet from time to
time, but . . .'

But Mandy had moved up in the world. Kemp could understand how it had been.

As if reading his thought, and deprecating it, Dorothea
went on, rushing her words:

'She wasn't snobbish. No one could ever say that of
Mandy. Why, in that awful office with all those salesmen

hanging about, she was the one who used to listen to their gossip...' She stopped, conscious of the fact that Kemp didn't know what she was talking about. 'What I'm saying is, I don't think the fact that Bernard was rich meant anything to her. She never thought of money like that—as something in itself. And anyway, she'd just finished her design course at the Art School and got herself a good job. She wouldn't give it up to sit pretty at home and be the perfect hostess Bernard wanted. Then her mother died, and Mandy found herself independent... That was when Bernard and she parted, but I know they stayed friends until he died.'

It seemed a logical enough turn of events to Kemp.

'And the second husband?'

'Derek? No, I never met him. I think he was an Australian. Mandy said he made her laugh. They had good times together, from what she told me. But it didn't last. He wanted to go back and live in his own country, and she didn't want to go. She had a career by then. She said Australia was a bright desert where the kangaroos had to wear white gloves on Sunday...' The words seemed to startle Dorothea as they came out, and she added, belatedly: 'That's what she said...'

Dorothea began gathering up the plates, fumbling. Charley came to her rescue. She's seeing her friend, thought Kemp, seeing and hearing her now as if she were in the room.

He said to her gently: 'I think your Mandy had a happy life. It was testified in Court that she had been happy. This illness, for perhaps that's how she saw it, would have brought an end... an end she couldn't bear...'

Dorothea responded eagerly, as if grasping at means of relief.

'Mandy watched her mother die of cancer. She couldn't come to terms with it. She went to pieces... The first time I'd ever seen Mandy really upset in all the time I'd known her. She felt guilty at not being able to nurse her mother, at having to send her to a hospice to die. We were seeing a lot of each other then, she seemed to sort of need me...'

For reassurance, for an old friend not only to sympathize but to condone, forgive. Again Dorothea's headlong words underlined what had been Mandy's need.

'She felt terrible but she couldn't do anything. It wasn't in her nature, Mr Kemp, to cope with it. Her father had died of cancer too, back when I first met her. All it had meant to Mandy then was the loss of her Art School course, there wasn't enough money when he died, and Mandy had to go out to work... But later she knew. He'd thought first of her mother, left her well provided for—he'd been prudent and very careful with his money, so that when her mother finally went, there was a great deal more than Mandy'd ever thought...'

There was nothing here to surprise Kemp. Everything fitted very logically together, even the manner of Amanda Egerton's death. Yet there was something in Dorothea's reception of it which seemed discordant. On the one hand there had been her obvious distress, but now there was almost relief, as if she latched on to the possible cause of her friend's suicide as a desperate way out for some dilemma of her own. Kemp, fairly used to summing people up without their being aware of it, had not considered Charles's wife to be a person of great complexity, and he would not have observed her so closely now had it not been for his slow realization that, for all her hesitant speech, Dorothea Copeland was herself a watcher, and a careful one. She'd never miss a trick, he thought suddenly, this wife of Charley's for all her quiet ways and deliberate simplicity. She has always been an onlooker, a spectator at life's little games. And what she observes she tucks away in her mind to pick over like the jumble she takes in for her charities.

It was not until they were having coffee, brought by Charles to the square parlour with its beige three-piece suite, light oak bookcase which held china instead, and the geo-

metrically-patterned wall-to-wall carpet, that Kemp spoke
of the letter.

'It wasn't addressed to anyone, and there was no signature, but there's no doubt it was in your friend's handwriting. It wasn't read out in Court but I managed to get a look
at it afterwards, and I've copied it out.'

Both the Copelands looked nervously expectant, like an
audience faced with a problem play. Dorothea put her cup
and saucer down carefully, and took a lace-bordered hand-
kerchief from the pocket of her skirt, a homespun tweed but
worn with a dark-blue jumper which matched her eyes.
Kemp was rather pleased to see that there lurked in her a
modicum of vanity.

The letter left by Amanda Egerton was not the kind anyone could read with a show of expression, so Kemp main-
tained a level tone, giving the words and the pauses between
their due meaning but no more. After a while he began to
feel like a newscaster, cool but sympathetic.

'''I don't think I can go on. I don't think now that I want
to know any more. It was a mistake in the first place me
finding out what I have. It's beginning to feel like it's eating me up. Malignant, that's what it is, malignant. The
whole thing's becoming a nightmare, the more I think about
it. It's what happens to other people, and then only in films,
and dramas on TV. My only excuse is that death has always
had a terrible fascination for me. It draws me to it. I do want
to know more but I can't face finding out anything else
about this body of mine. Useless to ignore it now I've found
out. I know I ought to tell someone else and get advice instead of driving out here tonight, and just thinking. My
courage is draining away. I can't stand any more revelations. I shall have to put an end to it now.''

'The letter broke off there,' said Kemp.

There was a silence as if they were all waiting for an echo
to die away, the echo of another voice.

'It was written on paper torn off a pad of good stationery, buff-coloured, Velvet Bond I should say... She used a ballpoint which was faint at the start, perhaps because it had been lying in the car and got cold. But after that the writing was clear—what they call an artistic hand, I believe, sharp downstrokes, short dashes for cross strokes...' He was only going on talking because neither of them was saying anything, and the gap ached to be filled.

Charles nodded. 'I've seen Amanda's writing on postcards and that describes it.' He turned his eyes on his wife. 'She must have known...that word malignant, Dot, it's dreadful but no one could have helped...'

Dorothea was looking at Kemp, though not necessarily seeing him. For the first time she had opened wide her dark blue eyes, and Kemp realized how beautiful they were, each iris streaked with purplish brown. He had not been aware of her eyes earlier, since she had a habit of lowering the lids when she was spoken to as if to avoid direct contact. Now she was staring straight ahead like a person in a trance.

He wanted to snap his fingers under her nose and say; 'Come back, little Sheba...'

Instead he asked her: 'Is that how your friend would write? Does it sound like Mandy?'

She blinked, coming back from whatever far land she'd been in. 'It's like hearing her speak,' she said, her voice husky. 'And that's how she writes—wrote. A bit dramatic...'

Kemp had thought so, too, but how otherwise does one write such a letter? One was not ordering new car covers...

More to break the brooding heaviness of the atmosphere into more manageable pieces than because he wanted the information, Kemp said casually: 'Did she know anyone called Frances—a woman?'

Dorothea shook her head. 'I didn't really know her friends. I met Rachel Freeman once—Mandy used her as part-time secretary when she was in the London office.

Mandy seemed to have lots of friends, but they were only names to me. I don't remember any called Frances. She went to Greece with somebody whose name was Denis but she didn't make a thing about it. And there was a man called Clive but she said he wasn't important...' Dorothea's voice had sunk as if she was talking to herself.

'Why do you ask?' said Charles.

Kemp didn't really know; perhaps because he felt that the conversation would otherwise die from inertia.

'It's just a little thing. At the top of that letter, where she'd begun writing and the pen wasn't working properly, when I held it up to the light there were faint marks. Looked like a capital "D" then blank, then an "F" and a small "r" and at the end of the word an "e" and an "s"...'

He heard Dorothea's indrawn breath, and was aware of her stillness. Charles turned to her anxiously.

'Dorothea?'

'I'm all right. It's just that...the letter...it was so like hearing her speak, the words she used...'

'I think I've upset you,' Kemp said. 'I'm sorry. Perhaps you'd like to have it?'

He tore the page from his notebook and held it out. She took it from him, glanced at it quickly, then folded the paper and put it down on the table beside her. She seemed to steady her hand with an effort as she picked up her coffee cup and sipped.

Kemp felt he could offer no further words. Her attitude worried him rather. She's tight as a coiled spring, he thought. Perhaps it's the onset of one of her migraines.

He could see also that Charles was at a loss for something to say. The air in the room was stuffy, the only sound a quiet clicking from the radiators as the heating rose to meet the challenge of a drop in temperature outside, the coming of a hard frost. From a vase on the bookcase, holding an arrangement of pampas grasses, and dried heads of hydrangea, a petal detached itself and fell on the carpet with a faint plop.

The hush was awkward, like the moment at a funeral when speech is inadequate, and no one knows what to say next... Which reminded him.

'About the funeral. It's to be at the Enfield Cremato-rium on Monday afternoon, two-thirty.'

'Thank you for finding out,' said Dorothea. 'I'd like to go—if you'll come too, Charley?'

'Of course I will, dearest. Wouldn't dream of letting you go alone. If that's all right with you, Mr Kemp? I'm com-ing back to the office in the morning anyway. I've been away long enough.' Charles saw Kemp to the door, and walked down the path with him.

'She's going to miss Amanda,' he said, 'not that she saw much of her, sometimes not for months. But they'd known each other a long time. You know what women's friend-ships can be like, they'd pick up the threads every time they met.'

'What did you think of Amanda Egerton?'

'I liked her. Everybody did. You couldn't help it. She was full of chat, and very entertaining. Odd that she should be a friend of Dot's, Dot's so quiet.'

'It can happen that way. Perhaps Amanda needed the stability of Dorothea's life to offset the hectic excitement of her own... The wonder is she never came to your wife when she was in trouble.'

'Amanda was headstrong. Dot used to say she brought trouble on herself by being too adventurous...' Charles shook his head. 'And she would never take advice.'

Kemp nodded. He was standing beside his car. Frost, diamond-bright, had already beaded the top, and he had difficulty opening the door.

'I've known people like that,' he said. 'Think they can run their lives like single-handed yachtsmen. But if the engine fails in mid-Atlantic, or your own heart gives out, the decision's taken from you. From what I've learned of your wife's friend, perhaps that's just what happened. She couldn't face the thought of someone else—even a doctor—taking charge of her life, so she took the decision to end it.'

Kemp knew he was venturing into the realms of hypothesis. He got into his car, not anxious to prolong the conversation; the woman was dead.

Charles leaned in at the window. 'We've taken up a lot of your time, Mr Kemp. Dorothea and I are very grateful. I'll see you in the morning.'

'Are you sure you can leave Dorothea?'

Charles had no doubts. 'She's fed up having me under her feet,' he confided. 'You know what women are like in their own home. She'd have me swept up in the Hoover in no time!'

He gave his dry chuckle, to which Kemp responded with a rueful smile.

'You know I don't have that problem. Charles. There are times I wish I did.'

As he drove off he glanced back at the house secure behind its private hedge, the warm light shining out from the porch. For a brief moment he felt he could envy Charles that snug and cosy sanctuary and the dutiful wife so much the mistress of it.

Dorothea had flushed when told of the small legacy that was to come when Mr Brunt got round to winding up the estate, and she had exclaimed, predictably enough: 'Why, that's a fortune!' Yet Kemp could have sworn she had only spoken as if it was expected of her, and that there were other things in her mind to which she was giving deeper attention.

EIGHT

THE NEXT FEW DAYS ran smoothly enough for Lennox Kemp—well, as smoothly as anything can run in a solicitors' general practice, which can never be entirely without incident.

Young Belchamber, cutting his milk teeth in front of a lady magistrate who had strong views on the sanctity of the home, and a dislike of her own sex—particularly when they dyed their hair orange—had his application for maintenance refused. It had been on behalf of a young woman teetering on the narrow edge between desertion and reasonable grounds for leaving.

'He threw her out,' he grumbled afterwards to Kemp.

'She said she was leaving and he didn't move heaven and earth to stop her. Get your facts right—especially before that Lady Bountiful of the Bench,' said Kemp. 'And next time, tell your client to keep her hair black, look pale and hungry and restrain her tongue. Appearance is everything...'

Tony Lambert raised his owlish head from a knotty problem in Trusts long enough to complain that the books on Equity in the small office library Kemp was painstakingly trying to establish were out of date. Kemp told him bluntly to raid Clements Inn, despite Tony's near-phobia for trains and tubes. 'It's only a City,' Kemp soothed him, 'it won't eat you, and if you take off those glasses you won't get mugged. Stay the night in Town and enjoy the bright lights.'

Michael Cantley had been on a loser in the Criminal Court, defending a burglar who couldn't have been more conspicuous breaking into premises if he'd worn a neon sign. 'Had to make him change his plea, then he'd the nerve to tell me he'd never been in trouble before. So there's me pleading mitigation with tears in my eyes, sick mother, broken home, give the lad a chance... Turns out he'd a record long as your arm, his mother's strong as a horse and works in the Co-op... Sergeant Dibble had a right laugh.'

'In which I'll join him,' said Kemp unfeelingly. 'Never trust a broken home, my lad, some very odd people have come out of them. You've only to think of Nero...Sergeant Dibble? That can't be his real name!'

Michael grinned. 'Well, you win some, you lose some. Actually it's Dibell. He might have warned me before I wasted my eloquence.'

'It's worth while having an early word with the arresting officers,' was Kemp's advice. 'They'll give you the low-down on your villain, and a broken home to them is only a house with the front door stoved in. But we're all supposed to be on the same side, remember.'

Only Nick Stoddart seemed pleased with himself. He returned from a morning in Court rubbing his hands with glee at having beaten into the ground an unfortunate plaintiff who'd had the temerity to accuse his employer of unsafe working conditions. Nick was jubilant, and ready to share his triumph with anyone he could corner in the Grapes at lunch-time. It was Kemp's misfortune to have slipped in there for a quiet sandwich.

'That scaffolding was safe as a nun's knickers,' Stoddart crowed, bringing over drinks which Kemp hadn't ordered, and certainly didn't want.

'Makes me go to sleep in the afternoon,' he remarked rather pettishly, trying to close his ears to Stoddart's detailed recital of the action, line by line, allegation by counterallegation, just as he had prepared it for Court—a recital in which modesty played no part.

'Give some credit to your Counsel,' said Kemp when it was over, game, set and match, 'he must have served a few aces to win that one.'

But Stoddart would have no other success but his own. 'He's nothing but a performing flea. I throw the bread and he jumps. He may be a good actor, but I'm the one that writes the lines.' There was too much of this braggart talk from Stoddart, until Kemp wished he could withdraw his own attention entirely, turn his thoughts inward and explore the wide caverns of his mind as Dr Johnson was said to have done when faced with an equally boring companion.

Any such retreat was effectively blocked when Nick mentioned Charles Copeland.

'...important contract to discuss and he's not even in the office. Now I call that slacking...'

'I gave Charles a few days off, Nick. He had trouble at home. You could have had a word with Tony if the contract was all that important...'

'Trouble at home, eh?' Stoddart gave a sly smile. 'Not with our Dottie, I hope? Thought those two were supposed to be a model of domestic bliss—if you like that sort of thing.'

Kemp decided to ignore the tone, and concentrate on the implication. 'You know Dorothea Copeland, then?'

'Of course I do. She was a typist at Gillorns years ago. That's where Charley met her. Rum little thing she was, like a pink-eared mouse. Quite bright, though. She left when they got married and she had her baby...I think I've got it in the right order, it was all a bit of a rush.' He gave a shark's smile as he cast the slur. 'You can understand what a temptation that five hundred pounds was for Charley—a lot of money in those days when you could get a nice little semi for a couple of thousand...'

'Have you remembered what that case was all about?'

'What case?'

'The one in which you say Charles took a bribe?'

'Why should I remember it?'

'It seems to be on your mind.'

Nick took a long swill at his beer while he examined the question for hidden snags.

'What does it matter?' He had decided to be truculent and unforthcoming. 'It's nearly twenty years ago, and a very dead file by now. Why'd you have to rake it up?'

'I'm not the one who did the raking. What branch of legal work was involved?'

Kemp's eyes had their uninterested look, but his tone was gently persistent.

'Oh, some kind of litigation... Insurance claim, I believe.' Stoddart spoke too carelessly for Kemp to be taken in. The man's put his toe in the water, he thought, now he's afraid of getting wet. Shall I go on needling him, shall I wait and tackle Charles himself, or shall I simply let the whole thing blow over? But sheer curiosity would never allow the last option.

'Which side was being represented by Gillorns?'

'The insurers, naturally... Always on the side of the big battalions,' Stoddart said, with heavy sarcasm. 'The kind of case we lawyers like best, the kind we can't lose.'

'What was the cast?' Kemp was keeping the needle in the same groove. 'Come on, Nick, you're the one who started this particular hare so you might as well stay the course.'

Stoddart looked surly. He was also beginning to get rather drunk. He pushed his chair back and went over to the bar. Kemp heard him ordering the day's special cottage pie, and another half-pint which he drained quickly as he chatted to the barmaid.

Kemp watched him with amusement, appreciating the act which Nick was putting on. I bet he's got the turbines of his mind going at full steam, he thought, but already they're a little clogged. And when Stoddart finally returned to their table with his meal, he had yet another glass in his hand, his face was flushed and the handsome mouth was slack.

'This business Charles was mixed up in seems to have made a deep impression on you, Nick,' Kemp remarked pensively. 'I can understand you being shocked at the time...but, after twenty years?'

'I told you. It was finding him out here, and hearing everybody sing his praises. Just wanted to set the record straight.'

'What was the case, Nick?'

Stoddart stared, his greenish eyes bulging. 'Wha's it matter to you?'

'It matters to me because I'm employing a clerk in a position of trust who may have been dishonest in the past,' said Kemp briskly. 'Now you know as well as I do that the Law Society takes a very grave view of any solicitor who doesn't check the credentials of his unqualified staff.'

Stoddart pushed aside his half-eaten pie and gulped his drink. Then he put his elbows on the table and tried to make a judicious point. 'That's only if they've got a prison record... Besides, you'd know nothing if I hadn't told you, old boy... Water under the bridge...'

'But you have told me. You have laid the burden on me. I would be failing in my professional duty if I did not henceforth more adequately supervise my clerk...' What absolute rubbish I'm spouting, Kemp thought as he listened to himself, what high-falutin' nonsense! All this happened, if it happened at all, years ago. I trust Charles Copeland, I've never doubted his integrity.

But that ferret curiosity deep in his nature was awake and starting to gnaw. Besides, Stoddart was rapidly approaching the stage when he wouldn't be able to distinguish between the Solicitors' Practice Rules and the Road Traffic Acts.

'So you see, Nick, why I'm anxious to have this matter cleared up... This matter which you have brought to my notice...' He waited until Stoddart drained the last dregs of his glass. 'What was the case?'

'Never thought you'd take it like this,' he grumbled, 'S'long time ago... Fire insurance claim...some office got burned down. Tottenham firm, name of Higgs... Higgs Electric...'

Kemp sat back. 'And we acted for?'

'The Edmonton Mutual... They were Higgs's insurers.' Nick Stoddart's memory for essential facts, a capacity which served him well in Court, surfaced now despite the effects of alcohol upon his judgement. 'Our clients demurred at paying up... Some question of negligence...'

'Thanks, Nick. And someone bribed Charles?'

'Never said that!' Stoddart tried a moment's belligerency, but it was short-lived.

'But you did say it. In my office. Five hundred pounds, you said.'

'Shouldn't have spoken. Forget it, Lennox... Forget...' Stoddart slumped over the table.

Kemp got to his feet. 'OK, Nick. Back to the office. At least you're not driving...'

Having seen Stoddart safely installed at his desk in the litigation department, Kemp advised his secretary to ply him with as much black coffee as he could hold. 'Mr Stoddart's been celebrating his success in Court this morning,' he told her cheerfully. 'Just don't let him loose on a client for a couple of hours.'

Then he went in search of Tony Lambert and caught him as he was reluctantly about to leave for the London train.

'While you're scrounging books from their library, Tony, will you do something for me? I want an old litigation file— twenty years old.'

Mr Lambert looked sceptical.

'We don't hold litigation files that long. Now if it was a Trust file,' he went on with enthusiasm, 'you'd have no difficulty.'

'I know all about the rules for keeping files, but I also knew Mr Archie. He never threw anything out unless the whole file had been thoroughly examined. There was plenty of space in the cellars, and he'd never spare the staff to do the sorting.'

'Since he left I understand there's been a great clear-out, Lennox.'

'That's as maybe. We might be lucky. It would be like Hercules and the Augean stables, clearing that lot out.'

He gave Tony instructions as to what he wanted, though he shared the young man's doubts. 'I pity whatever minion they ask to look for that file, and it'll take all day tomorrow to find it.' This pleased Tony, who was looking forward to burying himself in Gillorns' well-stocked library, and glad of the opportunity to spend some hours there.

It's a chance in a thousand, Kemp thought when Tony had left. Twenty years of legal business would generate veritable pyramids of paper, and in the cellars or attics of buildings a desert of dust—enough effectively to bury forever the bundle tied up with faded pink tape containing the pages, curled and yellow, of old correspondence, the Court documents stiff and dry, everything that had once connected Gillorns through the Edmonton Mutual Assurance Company with the little firm called Higgs Electric.

NINE

A WINTER ASPECT suited the crematorium, displaying its tidy symmetry by the removal of too exuberant natural growth which might otherwise obscure the neat pattern of paths and plots designed to calm the eye—and perhaps give ground clearance for the flight of souls.

Charles and Dorothea walked slowly, arm in arm, up the drive between frost-bitten flowerbeds and sullen stumps of rose-bushes pruned to within an inch of their lives, towards the red-brick chapel. A group of mourners from a previous service stood uncertainly in the doorway. Then, as if directed by an unseen hand, and conscious that they had had their allotted half-hour span, they straggled over to the one splash of colour where wreaths and sprays were arranged in the space provided.

Inside the waiting-room Dorothea looked around with nervous curiosity. She recognized the elderly man who must be Mr Brunt, the Collinses, man and wife, and the tall young woman in the smart hat whom she knew to be Rachel Freeman, Mandy's part-time secretary. The others—there were about twenty people in all—she did not know.

Clara Collins looked across to where Dorothea was standing, and gave a wan smile. Dorothea went over to speak to her.

'This is a sad day for all of us, Mrs Copeland,' Clara greeted her, moist-eyed and ingratiating, 'Who'd have thought it of Amanda? With her poor mother gone like that, too...'

'I remember,' said Dorothea, and she did, vividly. Those nights she and Mandy had sat curled up in front of the fire in the big old-fashioned sitting-room after one of Clara Collins's good dinners, laughing, gossiping, making plans. Had she envied Mandy then, Mandy who had that house and a couple of servants to look after her? 'I inherited the Collinses, like feudal retainers,' Mandy had said, 'and I mean to keep them in the style to which they're accustomed. As for me, I'm never going to wash another dish.' And, as far as Dorothea knew, she never had.

A middle-aged couple, she sitting tightly on a small chair, he standing portly behind her, were brought into the conversation by Clara Collins. 'Mr and Mrs de Lisle, neighbours of ours,' she murmured, 'and this is Dorothea Copeland who was Amanda's greatest friend.'

They both bowed, rather distantly. Dorothea wondered if they liked being called neighbours of the housekeeper and gardener. Did that mean the Collinses were to have the house? The de Lisles were well-dressed, and when Mrs de Lisle spoke it was in an accent which effectively removed them from any closeness other than the vicinity of their homes.

'Amanda has often talked about you,' Mrs de Lisle was saying to Dorothea. 'Why, only a short time ago she came to one of our dinner parties, and she mentioned you.'

'Did she seem...? Was she...?' Dorothea found herself stammering.

'She was her usual lively self, Mrs Copeland.' Mr de Lisle had a bluff, hearty manner, subdued for the occasion. 'You can be sure of that. Amanda was always good value at a party and never more so than that night. Sylvia and I have been devastated by her death. Couldn't understand why she'd do a thing like that. But after the inquest... Well, cancer is a terrible affliction.'

There was a movement in the doorway as the ushers gently herded—persuaded they would have put it—the mourners through to one of the chapel rooms. With a shuffling of feet and a scraping of chairs people settled themselves as if in church, although many had only childhood memories to guide them. Uneasy with these, they tried to reconcile them with present death, and fixed their thoughts on Amanda.

Dorothea too was thinking of Amanda. How she would have laughed. That's what Mandy would have done. She had always laughed. She'd even laughed that morning when everyone realized that Queenie was dead. Dorothea clutched her black gloves, fumbled with the book of the service so that Charles had to show her the page. And then the words seemed to have nothing to do with Mandy. Mandy who would have laughed out loud—even in church.

Dorothea had to admit that the Enfield vicar had done his homework; in the circumstances it was surprising how much he had put together of Amanda's life, and how carefully, piously but in no way unsympathetically, did he skirt around the manner of her death. He spoke of fear, of human frailty, and hope of forgiveness. Dorothea listened, as she had always listened, like an eavesdropper, her own thoughts running fast, unaffected by what she was hearing.

The singing had been thin, but it improved as they recognized the Lord as their Shepherd to a familiar tune. Dorothea's eyes pricked. She was aware that someone behind her had a rich baritone; not the one she guessed must be Mr Silbert, for he was at the front with Rachel Freeman, his sallow face raised heavenwards to show he knew the words and required no hymnbook, not Mr Brunt who was across the aisle, nor Albert Collins who sat with his wife under the lectern. Mr and Mrs de Lisle were on the other side of Charles, and Mr de Lisle had a pleasant tenor voice. Dorothea would have liked to turn round had it not seemed indecorous to do so. But her thoughts flew. Perhaps Denis of the Greek holiday? Or the irrelevant Clive?

The coffin silently, smoothly, slid away, and the curtains closed. Mandy was gone.

They bowed their heads in prayer, received the blessing, and there was a moment of quiet so intense that it held an almost tangible thickness. Then faces were lifted, throats were cleared and handbags retrieved. A murmur of conversation rose as they filed out. As the Copelands had been in the middle pews, others had gone before them so that Dorothea could only glimpse the backs of dark suits and a sprinkling of grey overcoats. From the front came Amanda's friends from the design office. Although they too wore dark colours they looked uneasy in them, as if their natural plumage had been clipped for the occasion.

The sun had come out, and pausing a moment in the porch, Dorothea was dazzled by it. Charles took her arm.

'You'll want to see the flowers, Dottie. What did we send?'

'I asked for pink and white carnations. Out of season, I know, but Mandy loved carnations.'

Someone spoke to Charles.

'Very nice service, I thought. Difficult in the circumstances...' He had a deep voice with a Northern accent.

Charles agreed, and they stopped to talk. The man raised his hat to Dorothea.

'It was my wife who really knew Amanda,' Charles said. 'They'd been friends for years.'

'I hadn't known her long. We met in the way of business. She was a very talented lady. She'll be greatly missed...' He was moving away when someone called his name.

'Clive? How very good of you to come.' It was Rachel who came over to them, holding her hat against a sudden breeze. They spoke for a short time before he turned in the direction of the car park.

'Who was that?' Dorothea asked Rachel in a rapid undertone, watching his back in the heavy dark coat.

'Clive Dale. One of our clients from Manchester. He's in the wholesale trade up there, and he's been very impressed with poor Amanda's work. I think they'd become friends in the last few months but I hardly expected to see him here...'

Without thinking, Dorothea broke away from her and ran down the broad drive to catch him up.

'Oh, Mr Dale?' She'd really no idea what she was going to say. 'I'm Dorothea Copeland...I wanted to ask you about Amanda...'

He had a ruddy complexion, and rather tired grey eyes in a handsome, fleshy face. His look was puzzled, but kindly.

'What is it, Mrs Copeland?'

'She mentioned you...' Dorothea was breathless. 'I had lunch with her only a few weeks ago, and she mentioned your name.'

He was waiting patiently for here to go on, but she didn't know where to start, and the words simply tumbled out.

'She said she went to the Cotswolds with you... One weekend. And I just wondered what...if she told you... Well, what you talked about?'

His face closed up, and he tightened his mouth.

'I'm sorry,' he said and, turning abruptly, he walked quickly away, leaving Dorothea standing.

You fool, she told herself fiercely, you utter fool. He's probably got a wife somewhere. He must have thought I was prying into his affair with Mandy when all I wanted... What did I want?

She walked slowly back to Charles.

'What was that all about?' he asked her.

'Amanda mentioned someone called Clive. I just wanted to ask him how she was then... If she'd told him anything...'

'About her illness you mean? She would hardly have told one of her gentlemen friends about that when she didn't even tell you. And I think from the way he spoke he was one of her gentlemen friends, and that he was very fond of her.' For all his quiet ways, Charles could sometimes be very perceptive.

'I think he took it in the wrong spirit. I didn't mean to sound inquisitive. It's just that . . .'

'Don't let it upset you, Dot. See, here are the flowers you sent. They really look very nice, and your little card. Shall we look at the others?'

There were a number of quite impressive wreaths from various organizations to which Amanda had belonged. Dorothea was surprised. All that world of business about which Mandy spoke so little.

She and Charles looked together at the floral tributes, at the petals so fresh, so innocent, at the black-edged cards wired to the stems.

'Good heavens,' exclaimed Charles, 'lilies! I didn't think people sent those any more. Who're they from?'

They both bent down in order to read the heavy black lettering on the white card attached to the great sheaf of white trumpets, their pallor greened by the ribbed veins.

Dorothea caught her breath, looked again.

To Amanda in memory. For I am not dead but sleeping.'

And the signature, from a strong and powerful hand:

'Queenie'.

Dorothea swayed. Charles caught her in his arms before she fell.

TEN

'THAT WAS a damned silly thing to do! What the hell came over you?'

The big man moved quietly like an animal on the prowl and the heavy carpet absorbed his tread, but the clatter he made at the built-in bar sounded his anger.

He shuddered at her laugh, raucous as a cockatoo. He'd never cured her of it. Her speech, yes, the years in America had given it a twang authentic enough. She picked up things like that quickly, took on character like clothes. There had been a blank sheet to start with, and the East London whine had slipped easily enough into nasal American, New York with just a touch of Brooklyn; well, she'd always been common.

She was already holding a drink, not her first.

'Can't you take a joke, damn you? Anyway, what's it matter?'

'It matters because someone could have seen it.'

'So what?' she snapped, showing her teeth. At least now they were expensive white dentures, not the yellow-stained points of her youth. 'Queenie would just be an old pal of the late lamented.'

'It was dangerous.'

'I like danger. I guess I've got used to it, living with you.' She yawned. 'Anyway, that little lark's over. Now, to business, has Cavendish signed the contract?'

'Not yet. He won't be ready for another two weeks at least. There's still a lot of negotiation to be done.'

'Do me a favour,' she drawled in the voice he hated, 'don't give me that. You've handled a lot worse...'

He smiled. Better that he should placate her. 'But it has to be done with kid gloves, here in England. And that's why I want you to keep out of it. Once we've sold up and the money's in our hands, you can have your head.' He ended, as he so often did, by wheedling.

She clapped her hands together, like a child, though there was nothing childlike about her. 'And we can buy that place in Hertfordshire, the one with all the acres, the swimming-pool and the gold bath taps?'

He never knew when she was putting it on; she had so many acts, so many accents. Had her dad really been someone on the music-halls, as she often told people? He guessed she didn't know, and neither did her mother, about whom she was equally hazy.

'You had gold bath taps in New York,' he said sourly.

'But this is little ol' England where there'll be tweenies to polish them, and parlour maids, and a butler I can go to bed with...'

He was seething inside, but he knew better than to let it show. If only she didn't have this crazy notion to settle here again. It was the rags to riches bit, that's what she wants to savour, he thought, and her ideas of England date from fancies bred in a slum... Not even from romantic novels. She'd never read a book in her life that he could see. Other people, that was what she studied, and my God, hasn't she done well out of it?

'We're going to live in the Home Counties, my darling.' She'd another voice now. 'And I'm going to play the lady of the manor.'

She's set on it, damn her. He temporized.

'After that last little episode, eh?'

'Lost your bleedin' nerve, have you? Well, I haven't and I'm not bloody well going to stay cooped up in here.' She glanced round the room with an expression of disgust. It was a luxurious apartment furnished to a high standard of up-to-date banality; beyond the long windows the trees of the Green Park waved gently, still leafless but the artless design their bare branches etched against the pale grey London sky shamed the room's contrived opulence.

He looked at her in despair, then was shaken again by uncontrollable rage. He could have hit her if it would have done any good, but he'd tried that before many times in their long relationship and had come off the worse; she would fight back with the instincts and fury of the alley-cat she was.

'You'll do as I say. My God, you've got everything here. What more do you want?'

She got up and went to get herself another drink. She turned at the bar cabinet and regarded him with narrowed eyes. She wore her black hair smooth now over the crown of her flat-topped skull and as she thrust her head forward he thought, not for the first time, how like a snake she was. But when she spoke it was softly through pouted lips.

'Only to go out and about... What difference can it make? I've got shopping to do. I'm back in London. It's my city.'

'Oh, go and buy what you like! You've money enough. A lot more than you ever had to your name when London really was your city.' He could afford the odd gibe now that she'd calmed down. 'And that's sentimental twaddle anyway. When you were last in what you call your city you hadn't the price of a decent pair of shoes.'

'Well, I have now,' she said with complacency, filling her glass. 'I'll go and get me some real crocodile.'

'Fine by me. But no wandering off. Stick to Bond Street and the West End.'

She grinned. 'What? No little jaunts to familiar haunts, tra-la? What a lark that would be!'

'Just don't try it,' he said grimly.

'Why not? I bet nobody'd recognize me.'

'She did.'

'Oh, come on, that was pure chance. And anyway it was you she recognized, not me. You haven't changed. Still the military man...'

'It's done me no harm.' It was his turn to sound complacent. He didn't need to glance at the mirror to know that what she'd said was true. Sandy hair took on grey unobtrusively, and although his features had thickened with the years their aquiline regularity still made him a good-looking man, and one conscious of his breeding.

'They love you for it over there, that and your awfully British accent. And to think you very nearly didn't come...' She was mocking him with what he knew she considered her gamine grin. She'd heard it said of her once, and he'd had to explain what it meant. Dear God, how ignorant she'd been! The thought crossed his mind that although he might have played the part of Professor Higgins, she'd never been an Eliza. It was she who'd taken the lead right from the start.

'You had to be persuaded,' she was saying, 'don't you remember?'

'It was a long time ago. And we agreed not to talk about it.' He said, crisply, 'I need another drink.' He crossed to the bar.

'Least said, soonest mended.' She talked in clichés in exactly the same way as she talked American slang. The common denominator. She had about as much depth as the bowl of a soup spoon, but the very shallowness of her nature allowed the thoughts to run fast in her head like globules of mercury in an empty tube.

It was true they never let themselves talk about the past, safer to keep it locked up in a box to which they both had keys but by tacit agreement never used. Neither had suffered by the arrangement, indeed the partnership in business—as well as the marriage upon which she had insisted—had succeeded beyond either of their wildest dreams. He would have deprecated any suggestion that they were two of a kind but in fact that was what they were.

And now the corporation they had built up together in New York and which had flourished like the green bay tree, was expanding to absorb other companies in this their native land, where the lure of their dollars had proved a powerful magnet.

It had been tricky, their return—at least it had seemed so to him, the more cautious of the two. But not to her.

'It's been twenty years, for God's sake! What're you scared of?' she'd exclaimed when the deal was being set up. She'd done the groundwork meticulously, striding up and down their New York apartment in much the same manner as all those years ago she'd strode the creaking floorboards of Higgs Electric, a grubby sheaf of salesmen's reports in her hand, exhorting, cajoling, hustling people, setting them at odds with each other, but always in the end getting her own way. She'd been only a spluttering firework then, energy striking from her like the sparks and bangs of a jumping cracker. Now she'd got that energy tamed, and channelled it so that the schemes and plans could pile up neat and tidy inside her head as if in a filing cabinet, annotated and cross-referenced for certainty, one step at a time— but such rapid steps as to take the breath away. She could take decisions in twenty-four hours which would take others weeks to think about.

There were times when even he who had known her so long could only stand back and marvel at her audacity. Such astonishment, however, did not stop him enjoying the fruits of her flair for business, nor crediting himself with the share he put down to his own accomplishments, his fine manners, his gentlemanly airs ... And my family money which launched her, he would think savagely at such times, conveniently forgetting how and why that money had been extracted from him in the first place. He was not a man given to any orderly reflection on the past. Such thoughts came only in spurts of resentment when she annoyed him—as she was doing now.

'Why can't we go out on the town tonight?' She was sulky, not altogether appeased by the prospect of an afternoon's shopping.

'We'll stick to the schedule. Dinner here. I'll have it sent up.'

She began to look mutinous. 'It's so boring...being stuck in this joint.'

He looked through to the dining-room, the black marble table already set with gleaming glass and silver. 'We'll eat here,' he said curtly. 'It's safer.'

'Well, what about the weekend? There's a fabulous place in Kent...'

'It's too much of a risk. Separate, we're OK. Together, there's still a danger. Come on, Quin, have another drink.'

Drink softened her, took the edge off that damned sharpness, made her more malleable. It was the only thing that worked. That, and sex... Invariably the one followed the other. He wasn't complaining—in fact he still found her exciting. That had been the surprise of his life, and the bond which finally cemented them together.

At first it had shocked him, for he'd never really liked her, at times hated her for the hold she had over him, but slowly it had dawned on him that he'd been awarded compensation. She was wonderful in bed—for all that she had no figure worth speaking of, a squat body and terrible legs, and, in those early years in the States before she discovered beauticians and hairdressers, she had no looks. A yellow complexion, pitted with the scars of acne, gaps in her teeth, heavy eyebrows and a beakish nose. But she'd gone to the right people, taken their advice meekly, and found that, although she'd never be an English rose they'd gone out of fashion anyway, while her own dynamic style, skilfully refurbished, was definitely in.

It had come as no surprise to her that money can buy you anything—she'd known it since she was a dirty child playing in a back street. And, it had been just her luck—not his—that the Bulett estate, tied up for years, should have been released so timely and so satisfactorily at such a crucial moment to serve both their needs. A little earlier, or a little later, and the Major—as she still thought of him—might have escaped her altogether.

'I guess what you have in mind,' she said now, getting out of her chair and going towards the bedroom. 'It's showing in your eyes...'

He followed her and watched as she slipped out of her dress, her underclothes, and turned to him, naked. At moments like these his doubts vanished. It had been worth it after all. Together they were terrific.

But today something stopped him, the normal excitement—just a fraction above pure lust—was stayed even as she looked at him, expectant and confident.

'Aren't you ever frightened, Quin?'

She had very round, very black eyes, nearly always totally without expression. 'What of?' she said.

He couldn't put it into words, not words that she would understand or respond to. Any conversation beyond the superficial needs of the moment would faze her, yet in the brash world of buying and selling in which they moved no one except himself seemed to be aware of it. She had prompt answers to everything so that she was considered smart—not without good reason. She scooped up information as she did phrases, like a bird pecking corn, and she used both with uncanny accuracy so she was considered quick-witted—again, not without reason. Only he recognized that these gutter wits were all she had, all she got through on; the rest of her personality was dross.

He wondered sometimes if she knew the difference between truth and falsehood, for she lacked the normal guidelines, yet she covered her lies so swiftly that she was rarely caught out; the rapid-fire manner of her speech simply increased her reputation as a wily, resourceful operator.

He was a pretty fair operator himself, and not given to unnecessary introspection as to the rights and wrongs of his own conduct, but the events of the last few weeks had disturbed him. He was vaguely aware that he was seeing her in a new dimension, although if he had cast his mind back—an exercise he preferred not to undertake—he would have found nothing new in it. But the speed and assurance of her recent actions had left him gasping, and, yes, afraid, even if she was not.

'What of?' she said again, pulling down the peach-coloured duvet on the bed, and settling back against the pillows.

He began to undress, more immediate need taking priority over thought. 'That we might have overlooked something,' he said, lamely, 'that some connection could be made...'

'Forget it, buddy.' She was always at her most American when making love. 'This is the only connection worth more than a dime...' She stretched herself to take the weight of his body, and murmured: 'Amanda whatever her name was, she's dead as mutton...'

ELEVEN

'I SUPPOSE Mr Stoddart told you.' Charles Copeland sounded as miserable as he looked. Although perched upright on the mere edge of the chair opposite Kemp, he nevertheless gave the impression of a man slouched in utter despair.

'I asked Mr. Stoddart to give me a reason for his hostility to you in this office.' Kemp was going warily, as if a single harsh word would cause the other man to disintegrate completely and he'd have to sweep up the crumbs from the floor. 'When he cast doubts on your character I'd no option but to question him further.'

'And he told you . . .' Charles repeated dully.

'He told me certain things, Charley. But I'd like to hear your version.'

'What's the use? Anyway, it was such a long time ago . . .'

'So everyone keeps telling me. I'd still like to hear from you.'

'So that you can give me the sack?' The old expression came sideways from Charley's mouth, wryly and with barely suppressed bitterness.

'That's rubbish, and you know it. Look, Charles, I'm not interested in tales out of school and I never did hold with sneaking. I should never have listened to Nick in the first place, but I did, and shall I tell you something? I have a weakness.'

He grinned suddenly, and there was something about that seemingly spontaneous grin which disarmed Copeland. Kemp was not without guile; he'd used that ready, companionable smile before and was well aware of its effect.

'I've a weakness,' he went on, 'for wanting to know the whole of a story when I've only got a part of it.'

Kemp stretched for cigarettes. 'You don't smoke, do you, Charles? Wise man. As I was saying, I suffer from chronic curiosity. It's a disease with me. Nags like an aching tooth.'

Charles slid back in his seat, but old habits die hard and he was still cautious.

'You want my side of the story, Mr Kemp? I think I'd like to hear what Mr Stoddart said first.'

'All right, if that's what you want, you shall have it.'

Kemp told him briefly the gist of Nick's remarks but avoiding any mention of the names in the case.

By the time he had finished Copeland's face was brickred, and his eyes were blazing.

'The bastard!' he burst out. 'The bastard!'

He pushed himself forward, and looked Kemp straight in the face. 'Oh, it's true all right, but he was in it too. Didn't he tell you that?'

'No. He did not.'

Charles was muttering to himself, coherent speech appearing to have failed him.

'Was Mr Stoddart also involved in this bribe?' Kemp asked.

'Of course he was. It came from him. He knew the man.'

'What man?'

'That manager. The one in charge of the firm. It was Stoddart he approached first.'

Kemp drew in his breath. 'Tell me about it, Charles. We've plenty of time.'

It sounded a sordid little tale the way Copeland told it, an episode long repressed, grown turgid with guilt in the memory; he blurted it out now in short spasmodic sentences.

Two young clerks handling what in a solicitors' office like Gillorns had been considered a very minor matter, an insurance claim for a burned-down building.

'It wasn't big money,' Charles insisted. 'They were only a small company, a subsidiary of a larger concern...' He closed his eyes and ran a distracted hand through his thinning hair. 'I can't even remember their name. Anyway, Gillorns were acting on the other side. There was some question of negligence... To do with faulty wiring, I think that was it...'

'Not that the fire was deliberate to collect the insurance?'

'Good God, no. Nothing like that. It wasn't very serious. Otherwise Nick Stoddart and me, well, we'd not have been handling it.'

'This manager fellow, the one who approached Mr Stoddart, what was his name?'

'I can't remember. Really I can't. Only that Nick came to me one day and asked if I wanted to earn a bob or two, extra like...'

'And you said yes?'

Copeland hesitated. 'Not right away. But Dorothea and I, well we wanted to get married. I had nothing except my wages, which weren't much at the time, and neither did she.'

'So you took the five hundred pounds? And Nick got the same?'

'That's what he told me, half each. But I never knew if Nick got his half... He never mentioned it again. I got an envelope addressed to my digs and there was five hundred in it in notes. It's my word against his, Mr Kemp, and he'd deny it. He'd never have dared bring it up if he didn't mean to deny it...'

'What did you have to do to earn this money?'

But Charles Copeland was staring at his present position, and not liking what he saw. 'Who'd believe me? Nick Stoddart's a big lawyer now, and could smash me down in words. Perhaps that's why he's doing it this way. Thought I might rat on him after all this time and wants to get his oar in first. Well, he's wrong there. All I ever wanted to do was forget the whole thing ever happened.'

'Did anyone else know?'

Copeland shook his head, but he evaded Kemp's eyes.

'Are you sure? What about your wife? Did you tell her how you got the money? Come on, Charles, she worked in Gillorns, too.'

'I had to tell her,' Charles admitted reluctantly. 'We were strapped financially, and we wanted a house. We'd been saving up but we'd nowhere near got a deposit. I had no choice but to tell her.'

'Was that before you agreed to take the money, or afterwards?'

Copeland swallowed hard. His anger against Nick Stoddart had served as a shield against some deeper misery. 'We talked about it, Dottie and me. I think it was before...' He stopped and gazed out of the window, struggling both to recreate and avoid the scene of twenty years ago. 'She said I should take it. I remember I was surprised. Dottie never liked underhand things... But it was a bad time for both of us, Mr Kemp...'

'I see. It was a great temptation you faced, Charles. I think I can understand.' Indeed he could, and sympathize, too. Desperate situations can lead to desperate measures being taken. Kemp had himself been similarly tempted when the hoodlums who held his own wife's gambling debts threatened not only her sanity but her life. How could he blame Charles and Dorothea? Hadn't Nick Stoddart hinted at a possible ill-timed pregnancy?

'What was it you had to do, Charles?'

'Such a little thing...' Charles was trying to excuse himself by minimizing the episode, but he felt Kemp's shrewd eyes upon him. 'Nick and I were preparing the papers to go to Counsel. You know the form. All the reports, from the assessors and the fire investigators, that kind of thing. All we had to do was lose a few paragraphs on the technical side, miss out some letters from the bundle. Slight changes in wording. It was old Mr Fenimore in charge of the litigation department at the time. You wouldn't know him, Mr Kemp?'

Kemp shook his head.

'He was getting on a bit, and he'd more important issues on his desk. I don't suppose he checked the brief very carefully, and if he had, well, we'd just have got a rocket for carelessness, that's all. As it was, Mr Fenimore never noticed, and the brief went to an inexperienced counsel who was young and not very bright, and he never noticed either—at least not until he was in Court, I suppose, and then it was too late.'

'So the insurers lost the case and had to pay up?'

'No skin off their nose,' said Charles doggedly, 'there'd only been a hint of negligence, and anyway the claim wasn't a big one.'

'But if the proper papers and all the relevant information had been before the Court, the case would have been prolonged?' Kemp persisted.

'That was the whole point,' said Copeland eagerly. 'That's what the company wanted to avoid. They needed a quick settlement... Now I remember, they were an electrical firm. I suppose it wouldn't have looked good if they'd been found to have carried a fire risk on their own property because of some small wiring fault.'

Kemp snorted. 'It's not unknown. What's that saying about cobblers' children being the worst shod? Were there any claims for personal injuries in this fire?'

'Gillorns didn't have to deal with any. I think the fire happened at night when the premises should have been empty.' He frowned. 'But there was a fatality. Someone in the office who was working late.'

Kemp raised his eyebrows. 'Wasn't there a claim, then, under the Fatal Accidents Act?'

'Not that I can remember... Mr Kemp, you have to understand how I've tried to forget this whole matter. I put it right out of my mind. I'm not saying I didn't regret what I'd done. I've felt guilty about it ever since. It... it seemed to make me lose my own belief in myself. But once it was done I was determined never to think about it again. And, between Dot and me, well, it was never mentioned between us from that day to this.'

'And no one else knew except you two, and Nick Stoddart?'

'No one.'

'And the man whose name you've forgotten, the manager of this electrical company. We can't leave him out.'

'He got what he wanted, I suppose. Anyway, it all happened years ago.'

'Why does everybody keep saying that?' said Kemp with a show of irritation. 'As if the past never happened. Sorry, just a philosophical reflection... Now,' he went on briskly, 'what on earth are we going to do about you and Mr Stoddart?'

'I don't know, Mr Kemp.' Charles Copeland slumped, as if his shoulders were again taking on a burden.

'I don't propose to make a big thing out of it,' said Kemp, picking his words with care, 'and I don't relish having any sort of a showdown with our friend Stoddart. In fact it would be best if we kept what you have told me strictly between ourselves for the time being. He may think he's achieved his object in merely casting a slur on your character, and he might let it go at that. It's possible he may be sorry he ever raised the matter at all. It could have been simple spite—though I don't consider Stoddart a simple man...'

'Do you believe me, Mr Kemp?' Charles broke in. His eyes looked tired, the pleading in them hard to resist. Against his better judgement, Kemp responded quickly; any hesitation would only reinforce the other man's doubts.

'I believe you, Charley—if it's any help. Now, will you do something for me? Steel yourself to ignore Stoddart's animosity. Get on with your job, and perhaps alter your attitude to it. Be a little more outgoing in your relations with your clients. It's a new world we're fighting out there, and we all have to adapt to it. Don't let yourself be done down by the likes of Jack Greggan, just tell people how much better your services are. And it mightn't be a bad idea to ask Peter Begg out for a drink one night, eh? Chat him up, blind him with the jargon—how much better for his firm if they stick with the devil they know—sorry, the solicitors they know—than someone new to the town who hasn't already tangled with the whims and foibles of Newtown's planning regulations. Good lord, Charley, you've been fighting your way through that particular thicket very competently these last three years. Make sure Peter Begg appreciates that.'

As a Samuel Smiles homily or a salesman's exercise in positive thinking the pep-talk had enough wind in it to take off as a balloon on its own—though privately Kemp felt it went a bit over the top in ordinary conversation, and was certainly not in his usual style; he never saw the selling approach as anything other than a con, no matter how felicitously framed.

But it seemed to have worked wonders on Charles Copeland.

His face brightened. He solemnly pledged that, yes, he would mend his ways, cultivate his clients, and be more firmly competitive. He would even brace himself to stand up to Mr Stoddart and, by ignoring what lay between them, show himself to be the better man.

He went out of the office as if in running shoes rather than the workmen's boots he'd arrived in, leaving Kemp to ponder briefly on the power of words. Chivvying Charley along the road to affirmative salesmanship smacked too much of the same *modus operandi* being put to work by himself, a notion he disliked. Still, it had done the trick.

Only when Charles had gone did Kemp reach into the bottom drawer of his desk and take out the untidy brown paper parcel containing the bundle of papers marked 'Edmonton Mutual v. Higgs Electric', and dated 4th November, 1964.

It was a good rule to listen to the witnesses first in a case like this before reading through the strictly formalized account; that way there could be no danger of letting slip any fact, any name, to warn that one had prior knowledge. Total ignorance was as good a start as any.

TWELVE

CURIOSITY CAN LEAD YOU down rabbit-holes, as Alice had found. For Kemp, a few days after his talk with Charles Copeland, it seemed to be leading him into the battle-grounds of the Crimean War. The narrow streets in the hinterland of Lower Edmonton, caught between town and marsh, blocked off at one end by the railway embankment, had been named to honour the struggle up the Heights of Alma, the victory of Inkerman, the hard slog to Sebastopol and the ambivalent incidents of Balaclava. They gave evidence of date, no more. Few were left of the neat little back-to-back workmen's homes originally built there; most had been swept away by industrial development after the Second World War, giving place to small factories and warehouses. Now even these were being rapidly overtaken by clean concrete chunks of modern offices, the industries themselves left huddled under the railway arches, smouldering in sulky dilapidation at their forced retreat.

Higgs Electrical Appliances Company had been at No. 54 Alma Street, and had consisted of a top-floor office reached by an open wooden stairway along the short corridor from a showroom straight in from the front door, and, down the same staircase, a large storeroom area with a tiny compartment off it housing washbasin and toilet. The office had been divided up by lightweight partitioning, and the windows were set high and narrow just under the roof. From the storeroom there was a back door to the loading bay at the rear, and stone steps down to cellars. The whole premises had been small, stingy even, squeezed as they must have been into too meagre a space.

Kemp had the plans in his pocket. No use looking at them now, for Higgs Electric was no longer there, but its parent company—bearing a household name—had expanded to fill the vacant plot with a building of that peculiar battleship design so prevalent in the 'seventies commercial thrust. Kemp guessed that originally the offshoot firm had been allowed to lease a bit of run-down property belonging to the larger manufacturing enterprise, and then left to get on with it. From statements he'd read in the bundle of papers, Kemp noticed that Higgs still relied on door-to-door salesmen as an outlet for their vacuum-cleaner sales, which betrayed a certain seediness about the firm, and the under-provision of office space confirmed his impression that the place had been run on a shoe-string.

At any rate, in March 1964 it had gone up in flames, leaving only the steel shelving in the basement storeroom standing, twisted but intact, and the charred beams of the rest of the flimsy structure leaning on each other like half-felled tree trunks.

The claim against the Edmonton Mutual had not been a high one. No other building had been affected, the firemen had seen to that. They had arrived promptly from their nearby station but by that time the wooden flooring was well alight, and the flames were leaping above the roof. It was only when they tramped over the smoking wreckage they discovered the body lying beside a blacked-out window in the upstairs office. They had been alerted at midnight and been told it was unlikely there would be any occupants at that late hour.

This information Kemp had put together from an early account in the bundle of papers but there was no need for further mention of the body in later documents since it had no part in the claim.

In fact, on first reading Kemp could see little reason for Edmonton Mutual to have contested the claim at all; it looked a very straightforward case of accidental fire, actual cause unknown. Even when the action went to Court all they had wanted was for the amount payable under the policy to be cut down because, they averred, there had been contributory negligence on the part of the occupier of the premises or his servants or agents. This suggestion had been put forward in several of the letters from the insurers, and strenuously denied by the solicitors acting for Higgs Electric who, Kemp noted, were a reputable local firm. Further references to negligence were scrappy and inconclusive—for a very good reason, thought Kemp grimly—but in the end Edmonton Mutual seemed to have dug their toes in, Higgs Electrical lost patience and brought the matter into the Court.

Kemp wondered who'd been sent on Discovery of Documents; a nice little job for the articled clerk. He would sit with the clerk from the other side, scrambling papers, numbering letters—if the other clerk was inexperienced, easy to put one over on him if you were smart. And there was no doubt Nick Stoddart had always been smart.

The brief to Counsel had been simply that; very brief. Listed the documents herein from which Counsel would see etc. Counsel to pursue the question of contributory negligence etc, etc. Sent to the set of Chambers in Queen's Yard sometimes used by Gillorns, given out to a Mr Adrian Spindle and marked by his Clerk at twenty-five guineas. Even back in 1964 that reflected the unimportance of the case, on par with a minor motoring offence. Kemp had never heard of Mr Spindle, and Kemp knew those Chambers well and had been around the Bar now for some twenty years. Mr Spindle therefore did not seem to have made any name for himself. He had been a fledgling who had never grown feathers.

Had it been the young Stoddart who'd sat beside him in Court? Riffling through the file: 'Sorry, sir, we don't seem to have that particular letter...' 'Which paragraph of the report would that be? Isn't it with your brief, sir?'... Bewildered, distracted Counsel, on stage without a prompter... Bending down anxiously... Agitated whispering while a restless Court waited. 'No, sir, there's nothing about that in the investigator's statement...' Terse words from an impatient Judge, opponents sitting back with complacent smiles... Alas, poor Spindle, time to quit, your case is lost.

During these meditations Kemp had walked the length of Alma Street, and been confronted by the corrugated iron fence of the railway. He went back and turned into Inkerman Street where he'd noticed a public house. The hard pavements, the brick, concrete and glass of the buildings, the acrid smell from the hidden industries, had all contrived to make him both hungry and thirsty. And there it was, staunch survivor of older days with its green tiles, shining mahogany door and swinging sign of a red-faced officer in a busby—the Inkerman Arms.

It was just after twelve o'clock, and the place almost empty. Ordering his half-pint, and waiting for his dish-of-the-day, Kemp chatted to the barman who was middle-aged and, happily, not taciturn. Yes, he was the landlord, he'd been there longer than he cared to think about, and seen some changes in the district he could tell you, and promptly did.

Without being much of a drinker, Kemp liked pubs. During long years of single living, particularly at a time when his job had meant ferreting out the sins of the debt-ridden and the deprived, he had used them as places in which to relax, worry over loose ends, or simply sit observing the flux, his ears open, his mind blank.

Somebody ought to write a thesis on the English public house. Not Kemp, of course, for he was much too lazy although his experience of them was wide and his view affectionate. From rustic Travellers' Rests in what remained of the countryside inwards through the vast hostelries for coach-parties dotted along the arterial roads, the Bricklayers' or Bakers' Arms standing stubborn where all else had been demolished, to the tall Victorian gin-palaces, left about the City for Dickens's sake, they each had their charm for him, and the Inkerman Arms was no exception. It had escaped the well-meaning hand of blunderers and remained what it had always been—a place of refreshment for the working man.

It was big, it was gloomy and, although there was a babble in the 'snug', the saloon bar was quiet. A few people were scattered about on the cracked leather benches among the brass-topped tables, some in corners too dim to be properly observed.

Kemp was grateful for the garrulity of the landlord, as Albert Gremson was to find a willing ear. Only slight pressure on the tap was enough to release a flow of reminiscence; the fire at Higgs Electric seemed to have entered into the annals of the parish and become more vital to its history than any Crimean battlefield.

'Went up like a tinder-box, it did,' said Gremson, polishing a glass and breathing on its bottom. 'You remember it, Mr McIlvey?' He spoke to a small, elderly man who had edged up the bar beside Kemp to enjoy a bit of conversation, and perhaps something more.

'Not me, Bert, I weren't around till after. Heard all about it, though.'

'What's that chap who worked there? Still comes in, don't he? The one on the darts team?'

'You mean Larry Lanscombe. He was storeman at Higgs. Works down at the timber yard now.'

'He still lives round here, does he?' Kemp turned politely to Mr McIlvey who was eyeing Kemp's glass hopefully. 'Can I buy you a drink?'

The old man assented with dignity.

'Larry's living in the same house he allus did. Down Balaclava Terrace, number 43. 'Tis the only one left, near enough, and it'll be gone soon if Council has its way.'

The remark set the landlord off in a lament for old times, and a curse against development in general, Balaclava Street in particular. A neat woman with once-blonde hair piled high appeared with a steaming cottage pie in a brown earthenware dish, and Kemp decided to eat where he was, perched on a stool at the bar, for the loud talking was bringing others into the vicinity and the ashes of the fire at Higgs began to get a good raking over.

'The Major came in the very next morning, didn't he, Bert? Proper upset, he was.'

'The Major was a gentleman,' said the landlord, 'came in every week with the Rotary. We had a dining-room in those days,' he explained to Kemp, 'not like now... That new lot from the offices—we're not posh enough for them. They go for smoked salmon sandwiches at the places out the Great Cambridge Road.'

'More fools they,' observed Kemp, 'this cottage pie beats sandwiches any day. Who was the Major?'

'Manager at Higgs. What was his name, now? Bulett, that was it... Funny, when you think of it for he was a military man...and the name suited him. He'd got Higgs going from the start. Drilled those salesmen like they was in the Army, but it got results. I reckon that firm would've got away to real success if it hadn't been for the fire...'

'The big company closed it down, and they were all out of a job, salesmen and all, that's what Larry Lanscombe told me,' put in Mr McIlvey.

'Was there anyone injured in the fire?' asked Kemp, tentatively since nothing had been mentioned on that score.

'Happened at night,' said Bert Gremson gruffly, 'but unfortunately there was a girl working late. She died in the fire.'

'Larry won't talk about the fire, will he, Mr McIlvey?' said one of the men. 'We don't mention it when he's around, and anyway it's all in the past now...'

The older man nodded. 'You see, sir—' he addressed Kemp whom he had appropriated—'they said it started in that storeroom. Larry'd been an electrician before he joined Higgs, and it was him fixed up the place, like.'

'So there might have been something wrong with the wiring?' Kemp's remark was made casually but he knew straight away that he'd blundered.

'Never believed that tale...'

'Larry was in the clear...'

'No way was it Larry's fault...'

'The Major wouldn't have a thing said against Larry...'

'Lanscombe's the best electrician hereabouts... I'm one myself, so I should know. There ain't nothing he can't fix, and he'd do it safely...'

'You be careful what you're sayin', Mr...'

The chorus of voices, and the glares he was getting made Kemp uncomfortable. Larry Lanscombe was obviously a popular member of the darts team.

'I'm sorry, I certainly didn't mean to imply...'

'Stranger to the district, are you?' asked the landlord, either to lower the temperature or excuse his customers' conduct.

Kemp admitted to being from Newtown, that final crowning glory of the developers' ingenuity, and there were nods of sympathy along with commiserative murmurings. 'You'd not know, then, what it was like here twenty years ago... How friendly people were, and the place so full of life... Now it's a desert—even the youngsters got doleful faces...'

Kemp could have bet that twenty years back there'd have been some old codger bewailing the death of the wartime spirit: that song about the hard times of old England would never end...

But more pies, ploughman's lunches, sausages and mash were being handed out by the brisk woman who had no time to talk, and the group set to work on the food, still muttering, not altogether appeased.

Kemp brought Mr McIlvey another drink, and allowed the old man to steer him to a corner table.

'You're interested in our Larry?' The pale eyes were watery but alert. 'I've known him since the missus and me came to live next door to him and his ma. 'Course we've been re-housed in the flats since then...'

'But not Mr Lanscombe?'

'Ah well, they'd bought their house so it's got left till the last. Matter of compensation...' Mr McIlvey made a vague gesture to indicate that Kemp would understand these things. 'We were Council tenants,' he went on, 'so they could knock us down first. But Larry'll get a good sum for his, he's done it up over the years, modernized it, like.'

'He lives in it with his family?'

The old man drew in his breath, pursing his lips. 'Never married. Even after his mother died. Funny, that... I've been told Larry was a great one for the girls once.'

'Before the fire?'

'You're the clever one and no mistake!' Mr McIlvey must have been well over seventy but he had all his wits about him. 'That's just what my missus always said. Mrs Lanscombe told her Larry was never the same after the fire. Kept himself to himself, and never a girlfriend that we could see. Of course, he's past forty now... Puts the kibosh on it, don't it?'

Kemp nodded, not wanting to disrupt the small recital, though he couldn't bring himself to agree with the sentiment. He was in the same unenviable position but at least he'd had one marriage, gone wrong of course, but putting him into the statistical average and, he liked to think, opportunities since perhaps not available to the absent Larry.

'What about this girl—the one who died in the fire? Could she have been someone Larry was attached to?'

'Naw...nothing in that. I only heard tell of it afterwards but she was no girl. Woman of over thirty, and never a looker, it's said. There were plenty of young typists about, pretty ones too, that Larry went around with in those days. Fellow I knew ran the cinema—it's a bingo hall now—he says Larry Lanscombe was a regular Saturday-nighter... And in the back seats, too...' He gave a growling chuckle of remembered bliss, his eyes awash with his own memories: perhaps of his missus, perhaps of some other short-skirted heroine in the spacious days before the war when all that mattered was the big film and the velvet darkness.

Kemp took him gently back to the present.

'What did Larry actually tell you about the fire?'

'Not much... It'd happened the year before we moved in. The missus and his ma got friendly like women do, though she wasn't an easy woman, Mrs Lanscombe. Methodist—' as if that explained all—'and kept young Larry on a pretty tight rein. Well, she'd been widowed and he was all she had. She were a bit snooty because they were buying their house. Fair took us aback, that did. Most tenants round about hadn't two pennies to rub together...'

Kemp could understand the McIlveys' feelings; lower-class tenants in the 'sixties were rarely in a position to enter the new property-owning democracy.

'Perhaps Mrs Lanscombe had money of her own?'

'Not her. She'd only her pension and that weren't much in those days. No, it was said young Larry'd come into some money. A thousand pounds, that's what he paid for it.' Evidently there had been considerable interest in the McIlvey household on this subject. ''Course it set them apart a bit—folk round about couldn't understand why the Lanscombes didn't just go on paying rent like everybody else.'

'When did this happen, their buying the house?'

Old Mr McIlvey thought in sets of years, accuracy wasn't to be expected of him. 'Let me see... We moved in at the New Year. They'd got the house by the spring, I know that, for Larry, he began painting it, putting the fences up round the back yard—mind, they needed it, but our landlord he were a right misery and nothing ever got done. A few years later the whole lot were taken over by the Council. That really put Mrs Lanscombe up on stilts, I can tell you ... We were only Council tenants, she was a house-owner! Poor woman, she died soon after. I'll say this for Larry, he's never the snobby sort. Quiet-like, never has much to say, but he's popular down at the darts club.'

'So I noticed.' Kemp laughed.

'Were you thinking of going to see him? He gets in just after six, regular as clockwork. I see him go past our block of flats ...'

'My business will keep. Another day will do. I've got to drive back to Newtown this afternoon.' Kemp was already feeling somewhat guilty at sitting so long in these undemanding surroundings, listening to an old man's inconsequential talk, succumbing to some obscure whim, following a trail that he felt to be uncertain both in its ultimate aim and its present direction.

A fire in industrial premises, a young man who would not talk about it but had a thousand pounds to give his ma, two other young men with a like amount... It was all petty stuff, hardly earth-shaking, and, as everyone kept telling him, it had happened twenty years ago... So what the devil was he doing here, wasting his time, valuable time to his clients back in the office?

He felt lazy, lapped in post-prandial inertia. The cottage pie had settled nicely in his stomach, but lay there heavily; if he'd been at home he'd have gone to sleep. As it was, however, he pulled himself to his feet.

'I'll just sit on a bit till Bert's ready to close,' said the old man, looking up at him. He had liked this stranger who looked like a well-fed teddy-bear and had thoughtful eyes. 'The missus is down at the supermarket, she'll not be home

yet. Could I know your name to tell Larry?' he added diffidently.

'It'll mean nothing to him, but maybe I'll be in touch.
Here's my card.'

Mr McIlvey squinted at it, took out his spectacles.

'A lawyer, eh? It's been a pleasure talking to you, sir.'

'And for me.'

As Kemp walked towards the door he felt the great stillness in the place. The men at the bar had long gone back to
work, the landlord was counting money at the till and acknowledged Kemp's departure with a casual nod. Apart
from the clink of coin and subdued murmurs from tables
still occupied, there was a hushed silence which reminded
him, incongruously, of an old-fashioned chapel. He realized he hadn't seen any women; perhaps they were all at the
supermarket with Mrs McIlvey.

Because his thoughts were running on these lines, when
he did see the flash of a red skirt he stared. She was in a
shadowy recess at the darkest corner of the room behind
where he'd sat with the old man. Even as he glanced away,
conscious that his look of surprise might be construed as
impertinent, she twitched the hem of the red skirt out of
sight. He had only a brief glimpse of a dusky jacket, and
something peculiar about her face—its whiteness perhaps,
or the lips which matched her skirt.

A prostitute. That's what she is, he thought. A lady of the
night. There wouldn't be much trade here in the middle of
the day. Well, prostitutes have to eat and drink like everybody else…and take time off. They work unsocial hours…

As he pushed his way through the heavy door he imagined that her eyes followed him. It made him uneasy. How
long had she been there, sitting quietly against the darkly
panelled wall, obscured from view? For he was certain she
had made no movement, had not crossed to the bar, had
taken no part in the to-ings and fro-ings of those in search
of lunch or drinks. Kemp was a fair observer, habit made

him notice people and their movements. No, whoever she was, she had not moved. He'd seen the drink in a tall glass on the table at her elbow. One drink, and she'd made it last.

There'd been a shower of rain, and the pavements now were damp and greasy. Under a lowering grey sky—the kind that seems to press relentlessly down on the rooftops—the streets looked mean and without colour, the faint red of brick, dun of concrete and slatey-blue of glass scarcely counting, unable to raise the drab monotone of the scene.

Kemp's mood underwent a rapid change. He had felt pleasantly euphoric in the Inkerman Arms, its ambience suiting his idleness, and he had enjoyed the vitality of the talk in there. Now he was oppressed, not by squalor—for there was little rubbish about—but by the very sterility of the area. Not a blade of grass, not a homely weed showed by line of wall or in the cracks between buildings.

He suffered a moment of black despair, not a thing that happened to him often but enough to know, in one split second, what it must be like to look into the pit. With him such moments lasted but an instant, and were indescribable; it was as if a hand clutched his brain, darkening thought, blocking out the corridors of communication. He had tried to explain them rationally. The nearest he got was that they occurred through a combination of circumstances, something external to himself, like atmospheric pressure before a thunderstorm, a sense of foreboding, not quite a warning, more an apprehension of evil . . .

He was a few yards into Balaclava Street. Instinctively he turned round, and saw, or imagined he saw, a glimmer of red vanish round the last corner. Curious, and vaguely disturbed, he retraced his steps hurriedly. There were a few people in the street going about their business, heads bent to the chill of the east wind, but no one dressed in black or red. Yet again he had the illusion, caught on the retina like an after-image, that his eye had just missed her disappearing down an entry.

He went back to where he'd been, determined at least to have a look at No. 43 Balaclava Terrace which Mr McIlvey had told him was at the railway end. And there it was, in a small segment of the old terraced cottages, some still with their front railings intact defending tiny patches of grass and the odd spotted laurel bush.

No. 43 had a neat wall and, instead of grass, a jumbled rockery out of which nothing was growing except an ancient laburnum, last autumn's withered pods hanging on it like dirty washing. It looked as if it had had a hard time growing at all.

The house was blank-faced, drawn cotton curtains at each window, eyeless, yet smug, the dark brown wood cleanly painted, plastic guttering, and a glass-panelled front door with a pint of milk standing on the step outside.

The pavement was narrow here so that as he walked past the house a branch of the drooping laburnum trailed on his shoulder, scattering dead brown leaves. Impatiently, nervously even, he brushed them off and in so doing caught yet again out of the corner of his eye a flutter of red, but when he turned to look properly, there was nobody up the long street.

He'd had enough of this place. He began walking briskly back to where he'd left his car in a busy car park on the Hertford Road. He had a craving for the bustle of the shops, the hurrying crowds, the sounds of traffic. As he walked he tried to shake off the feeling of melancholy which had so suddenly attacked him. It was the district, he said to himself, its lack of cheer, its air of despondency, its dismal, efficient blocks of buildings, planned without imagination... But, his head told him, you've seen worse.

She was just a prostitute, he muttered to himself, looking for business... A lone man, walking without purpose, not even carrying a briefcase, a solitary man buying drinks for a casual acquaintance in a bar at midday... Strolling about as if he'd nothing better to do, looking at shabby old houses ... A shabby, lonely-seeming man, over forty...

That was it. He'd been hit by that remark of old McIlvey's. It had gone right home, and something in his demeanour had made her twig it. That's why she'd followed him.

But cold reason told him he was wrong.

THIRTEEN

DOROTHEA WAS DREAMING of Larry the Lamb. They weren't in the office or even down in the storeroom; the setting of dreams rarely bore any resemblance to life, either present or past. Dorothea knew this because she often dreamed. She dreamed most nights of ordinary things, simple extensions of the day's happenings carried on in bizarre surroundings, large shops, spacious hotels, houses grander than she had ever been in. She had been told that such dreams were simply assimilations of everyday events, a sorting-out process for the loose ends which wouldn't fit into an orderly pattern. People she knew, or had known, were never important to her dreams except as interchangeable faces which came and went to no purpose. She had also been told that her type of dreaming was healthy and showed she had a stable personality, free of neurotic fancies. She would like to have believed this.

But now she was dreaming of Larry, a persistent Larry who wouldn't go away... He was following her up a marble staircase, at her side along a wide corridor, holding doors open for her, trying to talk to her, but of course this was impossible since her dreams were as silent as movies in the 'twenties.

Dorothea woke, heavy-headed, trying to snatch at one of the rapidly disintegrating images. She had been told that if you held on to the least little tangible outline, then the rest would follow if you concentrated hard enough. She did so want to find out what Larry wanted... what he was trying to tell her...

Charley Copeland yawned, and reached out to turn on the seven o'clock news. The radio announcer's voice came loud and clear, scattering the fragments of her dream, and Dorothea knew Larry had scuttled back into the shadows, perhaps for ever...

But he came back in the daytime. Leaning over the sink, her hands in the sudsy breakfast dishes, she looked out of the window. It was raining. It did not stop Larry smiling in at her. How could anyone of such low-grade intelligence have been so handsome, she thought? All that soft black hair and those deep grey eyes that should have had more behind them than mere laughter and lechery.

Of course during her first months in that wretched office he had not been for her—she an awkward girl out of a single-sex school and trailing its precepts all too obviously about her. There were plenty of prettier, more worldly-wise typists in Higgs Electric or in the company next door for Larry to play around with. Dorothea had simply stood on the side-lines and watched with an envy which sickened her.

The only child of elderly parents, surprised in their middle years by this gift of a daughter—hence her name, meaning gift of God—Dorothea didn't know how to talk to boys, never mind grown men. If it hadn't been for Mandy she might never have realized that she was living in the swinging 'sixties, and even now when she read of that supposedly permissive society Dorothea curled her lip. She had never swung with the times, though the throb of that music still had the power to make her cry, perhaps for lost innocence... And that was a great foolishness for in those days she had thought her innocence stupid and been only too eager to lose it.

Dorothea sat down to her morning coffee determined to banish Larry from her thoughts and be truthful with herself. She had to admit that any memories conjured up by a Beatles' record heard on the radio or the sound of a rock group belting out old familiar numbers also brought with them the painful things she had tried to shut away. Since Mandy's death, that door was opening up again... And now Larry was standing behind it, trying to tell her something.

She got up hastily, and began to do the vacuum-cleaning. Then she would wash the white paint of the window-frames—they never stayed clean long in Newtown, despite the designation of light industry only—and make the dinner.

But the past was back with her now, with a vengeance.

How miserable she had been in that office until the coming of Amanda! Nervous as a mouse in a corner beside the blacked-out window, she had struggled with an ancient typewriter, frozen with fear lest the telephone bell should blare its message from the infernal box beyond her desk and she must cope with it, fumbling the falling dolls' eyes, the nest of serpents' heads she invariably plugged wrong, terrified when the Major strode out from his sanctum behind the partition, shouting: 'What the hell's going on?'

He had been kind enough to her at the interview, had found her qualifications adequate, and then proceeded to mystify her with the complexities of the work expected of her. The wages he offered had not been at all adequate; the secretarial college she'd just left would have warned her to ask for more. Dorothea had never in her life asked for more of anything. It was her first interview for a job, and she was determined to get it. She was equally determined not to fail at it.

And she would have failed had it not been for Amanda. She had decided to leave, a few days after Miss Mangan—Dorothea could never bring herself to call her Queenie in that spirit of false camaraderie engendered in the office—announced that the Major was taking on another shorthand-typist. Everyone there would guess it was because she, Dorothea, had been found wanting, not able to deal with the telephone machine, not brazen enough to beard the salesmen in their noisy den and get them to fill in their returns, scared to go down to the stores where the two ribald lads under Larry Lanscombe fell about in hysterics when she didn't know the difference between male and female plugs...

Dorothea had tried to come to terms with her failure, and brooded resentfully on its cause: Queenie Mangan. For Queenie was something Dorothea had never come up against before, a creature spawned in the East End of the City, her origins as obscure as her accent, sometimes the speech of the streets with its bawdy undercurrents, at other times an affected upper-class lisp at odds with her wide mouth and the gaps in her yellowed teeth. Queenie was all things to all people; a clowning maverick to the men, both the sworn confidant and the corruptor of the girls, she wielded her power with an uneven hand to divide and rule, thereby keeping the staff in a continual state of uneasy flux. Although she seemed to have no named position in the hierarchy of the firm, she was its mainspring, and the office revolved round her quick competence and knowledge. For Queenie knew everything—from the precise wording on the company's Articles of Association to the exact location and status of Major Bulett's two alleged wives.

She had taken against Dorothea from the start, called her 'Lidy Dorothy' in mock-Cockney, or 'Miss Prim' when Dorothea found it impossible to laugh at Queenie's grubby jokes which were always at someone's expense, or when Dorothea wouldn't join in the various little office feuds set up by Queenie. At first Dorothea simply feared the older woman's tongue, then fear turned to hatred—a novel and unwelcome emotion for a young girl of Dorothea's upbringing.

Fear and loathing dominated my days, she thought now as she swept the stairs. And it was Amanda who came to my rescue.

For Amanda was a match for Queenie. 'She's just a rat up from the gutter,' she told Dorothea a few weeks after they'd met, and were sitting in The Hub café exchanging office gossip. Dorothea had poured out her heart to Amanda, and Amanda had taken it all in her stride.

'Ignore the woman,' she said, 'she's the kind that has to have victims to tear with those awful teeth. She's marked you down as one. Don't you let her. You stick with me and you'll be all right. Look, I've got tickets for the *Six-Five Special* next week. Want to come?'

Amanda knew everybody in the free-wheeling teenage society about to come to the boil; who was having the best all-night parties, where to get free seats for shows, which pubs didn't worry whether you were eighteen or not . . .

And Amanda spurned the office. 'It's just a waiting-room,' she said, 'there's another world outside.'

Into that new, exciting world she took Dorothea along with her. As a foil? Dorothea didn't care. Dorothea put on sophistication like new clothes that weren't quite her size and in which she was uncomfortable . . .

But in the end she got Larry the Lamb. Got him away even from Mandy. That's what she had thought at the time. But now she knew Mandy had merely handed him on when she'd finished with him . . .

Dorothea felt herself grow hot. She poured the dirty water from the windows down the sink with an angry movement that splashed it over the rim. I must not think about Larry, she told herself firmly. But his face was there in front of her, no longer smiling, but desperately pleading: 'You won't ever tell, will you, Dottie? Promise you won't?'

She'd promised. How could she help it with her involved as well? She'd gone further. She'd told no one that she'd ever worked at Higgs Electric.

'That's downright silly,' Mandy had said. 'What did it matter? It wasn't anything to be ashamed of. I know it was a trashy place to start in but we couldn't help that.'

'It was just a misunderstanding,' Dorothea had told her lamely, 'when I went for the job at Gillorns. I said I'd worked for that solicitor in Enfield, Mr Allardyce . . . Well,

I'd been there temporary for a couple of months and he gave me a good reference so there wasn't any need to say where I'd been before.'

'And you've never even told Charley?' Mandy had opened her golden-brown eyes in astonishment. 'What a funny old slyboots you are! You're an inverted snob, you know. That's what it is. You want your new boyfriend to think you were never associated with such riff-raff as worked down Edmonton way...' Then she'd laughed and patted Dorothea's cheek. 'Don't worry, Freckles, I'll not spill the beans.'

So it had become their secret, a secret kept from Charles, but only a little meaningless one at first. For all Dorothea had wanted then was to forget, put right out of her mind everything that had happened at Higgs, her own failure to cope, the nastiness of Queenie Mangan, the awful bullying Major... and Larry. She had given a promise to Larry. No one must ever know about that.

Dorothea made her afternoon cup of tea and set it on the kitchen table. Scenes from the past were coming back to her now with a vividness which made her tremble. She put a hand across her forehead. A migraine coming? Stress, the doctor had told her, brought them on. She took one of her tablets. This wasn't stress, just the pressure of images as in dreams, but why were they here in the daytime, why was Larry here when she had shut him out for so long? The answer stared her in the face as clearly as did his eyes. Because Amanda had brought him back, and Amanda was dead.

FOURTEEN

IT WAS NEITHER the best of times nor the worst of times, thought Kemp, sifting through the morning mail, so why was he in this curious mood of despondency? Head Office had been pleased with his report on the comparative departmental costs, and placated for the time being by his explanation on conveyancing—fresh blood competing in the district and a few clients finding it temporarily to their taste, the rise in house prices locally making the younger element hesitant about that larger place they'd had their eye on, the slack season of the year...

But Kemp had noticed there was a spring in Charles Copeland's step, and a revival of keenness in his work. Brown Bros. were back in the fold with instructions on their new housing estate. Stoddart had been out of the office a lot, perhaps in court, perhaps, Kemp hoped, looking for pastures new, fresh fields to conquer, and if so, he wished him luck.

There was nothing in the correspondence either to give Kemp cause for concern, just the usual matrimonial acrimony, opposing solicitors doing their job, taking up battle positions under the old adversarial process. Why, he reflected, indulging his present mood, did the common law of England have to develop from the concept of man against man in single combat, and spill this alarming pugnacity over into the delicate issues of marital dispute?

Later, Elvira commented when she came to see if he'd finished doing a tape for her: 'You're a bit glum today, Mr Kemp. Is anything wrong?'

'That's the trouble. I think there is but I don't know what or where...'

'You ought to be pleased with yourself,' she went on. 'You've won that maintenance claim for Mrs Evans, Walters v. Walters has been settled out of court, and Mrs Booth's decree absolute's in this morning so she can get married on Saturday as she planned. I don't see what you're so gloomy about.'

Neither did Kemp, yet his spirits showed no signs of rising nor could he shake off the uneasy feeling which he had tried—quite inadequately—to express to Elvira. He could trace it back to the oppression which had come upon him suddenly as he left the Inkerman Arms yesterday afternoon.

He worked hard till lunch-time and was preparing to leave the office when the phone rang.

'Lower Edmonton police station on the line for you, Mr Kemp.' He picked up the outside line.

'Is that Mr Lennox Kemp?'

'It is.'

'I wonder if you could come in and see us, sir?'

'What about?'

There was a pause.

'Station Sergeant Lucas here. It's concerning a death that has occurred in this district. Man by the name of Lawrence Lanscombe.'

Kemp's stomach gave an unpleasant lurch.

'Why are you calling me?'

'Well, sir, I understand your card was found at the house. Detective-Inspector Inskip wondered if you could come to the station—if it's convenient.'

'How did this man die?'

'I'm not at liberty to say, sir.'

Kemp thought rapidly. 'I was just going to lunch. Tell DI Inskip I can be with him in about an hour's time.'

'Thank you, sir.'

Kemp replaced the phone slowly. He put his elbows on the desk and stared at the blank space of wall between two filing cabinets. That's it, he thought, the sin of omission. It's been nagging at me, something I left undone. I should have trusted my instinct. Instinct told me to follow it up... But I couldn't have foreseen...

He went for his car, and drove towards London.

The police station was in a side street just off the Hertford Road. It was new, and bright, and busy. The desk sergeant rang through, and indicated that Mr Kemp should go straight in.

Detective-Inspector Inskip was young, fresh-faced and tight-lipped but he greeted Kemp with courtesy.

'Good of you to come right away, Mr Kemp. I know how busy you lawyers are.'

Kemp seated himself in front of a tidy desk, and Inskip wasted no words getting to the point.

'A Mr Lawrence Lanscombe was found dead this morning at his home, number 43 Balaclava Terrace. We found your card lying on his kitchen table.' Kemp could see it now on the Inspector's blotting-pad.

'How did the man die?'

'Looks like an accident...or possibly suicide. We have to make inquiries, you understand, and your card was there.'

'I see. When was he found?'

'The milkman's in the habit of leaving a pint of milk every morning about half-past eight. Normally Mr Lanscombe's gone to work by then. This morning his light was left on—it's a glass door and you can see right through to the kitchen. The milkman thought there was someone at home so he called through the letter box. Then he smelled gas. He did the right thing. Phoned us from a neighbour's. We broke into the premises. There was gas everywhere, an unlit oven, and Mr Lanscombe slumped on the floor. The neighbour confirmed it was him. He was quite dead...been dead some time. The doc says at least eight hours but of course the post-mortem will confirm cause and time of death. And that's all we know...'

Kemp nodded at the card. 'That was lying on the table?'

'It was the only thing there except for an empty whisky bottle and a tumbler. Otherwise the place was tidy. If he'd had a meal earlier in the evening the dishes were washed up and stacked on the draining-board. Now, Mr Kemp—' the Inspector clasped his hands together below his chin and looked at Kemp over them—'can you throw any light on this matter?'

Kemp took his time answering. He was used to being evasive with the police when necessity arose and when duty to a client impelled caution, but in the present circumstances he had no client and was undecided where his duty lay.

He came to the conclusion that half-truth would do no harm.

'I have never met this Mr Lanscombe, Inspector,' he said carefully. 'As you see, I work at Gillorns, solicitors of Newtown—many miles from here. I had occasion recently to go through a bundle of old files, part of a sorting-out process before throwing them out. All solicitors have to do this from time to time, particularly these days when office space is at a premium.'

He glanced round the tidy room at the neatly arrayed files and card indexes, everything strictly functional and in apple-pie order, and guessed all records here would be computerized.

'Paper's the bane of a lawyer's life—' he gave the Inspector an engaging grin—'and we can't keep stuff that's twenty years out of date... Anyway, one of the cases concerned a fire that happened down Alma Street ages ago, and after I'd been to see a client in Edmonton yesterday morning I thought I'd go down there and have a look at the place. Of course it had gone. Well, twenty years is a long time in industrial development... I went into the Inkerman Arms for a spot of lunch and got talking to some of the men there. One old gentleman said a Mr Lanscombe had worked at the place where the fire was. I think the old man was a bit lonely and wanted a chat, so I bought him a drink and he talked about Larry Lanscombe—as he called him.'

During this somewhat sketchy recital the Inspector had been watching Kemp with small sharp brown eyes. He didn't look like a man who would be easily taken in, but Kemp had made sure there was nothing in his story which diverged too flagrantly from the truth; Mrs Booth of the eagerly-awaited decree absolute did work in a shop in Edmonton and he might well have called upon her to advise patience.

'So you were interested in Mr Lanscombe?' Inskip had grasped the point.

'Not really...' Kemp confessed, sitting back in his chair and crossing one leg over the other, 'I'd never even heard his name until Mr McIlvey mentioned it. That's the old gentleman, by the way. He told me he lives in one of the Council flats near here.'

'If you weren't interested in Mr Lanscombe, then how did your business card get to be in his house?'

'I can only imagine Mr McIlvey took it there.' Kemp put on his most vacant expression. 'As I said, I think he was glad to find somebody to chat to. For myself, I was simply passing an idle moment... But the old man had given me his name, it seemed only polite to give him mine when he asked for it, and I had a card on me. I did tell him that it would mean nothing to Mr Lanscombe. He'd no more heard of me than I of him until yesterday.'

Inskip kept rubbing his thumb across his lower lip. His eyes hadn't moved from Kemp's face. It was plain he wasn't satisfied but he couldn't find a handle to twist in anything Kemp had said, and he was well aware he was dealing with a lawyer.

'I shall have to see this Mr McIlvey,' he said at last, getting to his feet, 'and I shall probably have to be in touch with you again.' He paused as Kemp rose also. 'Just a minute, Mr Kemp. What was this place that had the fire?'

Mr McIlvey would tell him soon enough, no point in stalling.

'A firm by the name of Higgs Electric Appliances. But you'd be just a lad at the time...' Inskip was a very young inspector.

Leaving the police station, Kemp glanced quickly at his watch. Just after two. If he hurried he might get to the Inkerman Arms before it closed.

Landlord Albert was not pleased to see him, nor was there any welcome for Kemp in the lowered glances of the men grouped round the bar, some of whom he recognized from his previous visit. There was quite a crowd considering the time, the news had obviously spread and taken precedence over work. There was no sign of old Mr McIlvey.

Kemp ordered a half-pint of lager which Gremson put down on the bar-top without a word—and just out of reach so that Kemp had to stretch an arm for it. There was a silence thick enough to bite, then a growling murmur form the far end of the counter. Slowly, one or two men detached themselves from the group and moved towards Kemp; they seemed to have been picked as front persons...

'You caused trouble, mister,' said one.

'Coming in here yesterday like you done, and sounding off about Larry Lanscombe...'

'They found Larry dead this morning, did you know that? Gassed hisself, it's said...'

Kemp remained quiet, stood his ground, taking a long, slow drink. What do they think this is, he thought with a spurt of hilarity, a shoot-out at the OK corral? He was aware of Gremson's careful eyes watching him.

'What we want to know is, what did you have to do with it?' The thick-set man with reddish hair who had spoken last sidled up and leant on the bar at Kemp's elbow. He stared slantwise into Kemp's face with angry bright blue eyes.

Kemp took no notice.

'You want to watch it, mate, comin' here askin' questions. What you'll get's trouble all right . . .' A large man in workmen's clothes pushed into Kemp from the other side bunching his fists like knuckles of ham.

Kemp slid his empty glass gently back across the bar-top, and turned round. Half a dozen of the men looked menacing enough, the others were onlookers.

He addressed those closest to him but spoke loudly so that all could hear.

'I know that Larry Lanscombe was a friend of yours, and I am very sorry for what's happened, but I give you my word I did him no harm. I had never met him, and hadn't heard of him until I came in here yesterday. I am a solicitor,' he went on, enunciating each word with studied clarity as if giving a lesson to children, 'and my only interest was in that fire at Higgs—an old insurance claim that's dead and forgotten. Mr Gremson here will vouch for me that I never mentioned Mr Lanscombe's name. Isn't that so, Mr Gremson?'

Grudgingly, the landlord admitted that it was.

'You were out to blame Larry for the fire,' the thick-set man muttered. 'I heard you with my own ears.'

'You did not,' said Kemp sharply. 'I mentioned faulty wiring. It was you who took it up. I brought no trouble on your friend, believe me. As to how he died the way he did, that's for the police to find out. And I'm as anxious as they are to discover why.'

It was good court-room tactics to speak out clearly, distinctly, and with the intention to be heard, overriding any murmurs of dissent. For all his normally diffident manner, Kemp had a strong voice and knew how to use it. His firm tone and the seriousness with which he spoke began to affect his audience, and he was quick to take advantage.

Give them something solid to work on, get their slow minds moving so that they'll stop thinking with their feet. . .

'Did any of you see Mr Lanscombe last evening?'

There was a chorus.

'He were on the darts team as usual.'

'Played in the match here, didn't he?'

Bert Gremson was the most coherent.

'Larry was here last night till half-ten. Played like a wizard, couldn't put a dart wrong.'

'When did he leave?' asked Kemp.

'Like I said, half-ten.'

'Anyone go out with him?'

The red-haired man had stepped back from jostling Kemp, and answered mildly now that he'd been given something concrete to fix his attention on.

'I walked to the corner of Alma Street with Larry, same as I allus does...'

'And he was his usual self?'

'Better'n usual. He'd played a blinder. Won that match for us.'

'Did he have much to drink?'

'Naw. You can't aim a dart when you've taken on a load.' This came scathingly from one of the younger men. 'Of course after the match was over we all had a few...'

'About normal,' Gremson said to Kemp, 'after all, they'd been celebrating. Nothing wrong in that. But Larry's never been a great drinker. He was cheerful, though. I remember him calling out good night as he went out the door. He wasn't always so cheery, Larry, got depressed at times... Well, who wouldn't, living alone in that house. Stands to reason.'

There was a general mutter and shaking of heads which seemed to indicate, somewhat perversely, agreement with the landlord's view.

'Mr McIlvey's not in today?' Kemp observed.

'Haven't seen him. He'll take it bad, he and his missus. They've known Larry longer than most.' The thick-set fellow was by now almost friendly so that he answered without hesitation when Kemp asked him where the McIlveys lived.

'Nightingale Court, down the far end of Sebastopol Street. Ground-floor flat. She's arthritic, Mrs McIlvey. You'll not go bothering them?' he added, anxiously.

'Not today,' said Kemp firmly, reflecting that the police would be doing just that. 'When I do see him it will only be to offer condolences. I rather took to Mr McIlvey, and I've no wish to cause him further distress.'

The landlord was gathering up glasses. He looked meaningfully at the clock above the bar, and the men began to drift towards the door, but reluctantly, as if work held little attraction for them today.

Kemp called after them. 'I'm obliged to you gentlemen for your forbearance. I'm sorry we seemed to get off on the wrong foot at first...'

'That's all right, mate, no hard feelings. Suppose you were just doin' a job like the rest of us.'

When the last one had trailed out Kemp turned to Mr Gremson.

'I shan't keep you a moment, but there's something I wanted to ask you. You keep your eyes open in this place. Do you remember a woman in here yesterday? She was over in that corner behind where Mr McIlvey and I were sitting...'

Bert nodded. 'I seen her. Black coat, red skirt. Gin and tonic with ice and lemon. Just the one.'

'Prostitute?'

Bert was horrified. 'In here? You must be joking. This is a working men's pub not one of your fancy lah-di-dah places.'

'Sorry. Was she a local woman? I mean, did you know her?'

'Never set eyes on her before. A complete stranger—like yourself, if I may say so. Will that be all? I got to close up.'

'Thanks, Mr Gremson. You've been a great help. I hope this sorry business of Mr Lanscombe gets cleared up.'

Gremson grunted. 'Won't bring him back on the darts team, will it?' he said with morose truth as he followed Kemp to the door. He swung it shut with a bang behind his customer, and shot the heavy bolts.

Well, at least I got on to the team before the police, Kemp thought as he walked down the street. It wasn't much consolation. He felt drained. He had been keeping himself on a tight rein both during his interview with the Inspector and back there in the Inkerman Arms; there had been so much he wanted to know yet he'd had to tread a careful path. Now real misgivings assailed him; despite the certainty he'd tried to convey to the men at the bar that he had not been the one to bring trouble on Larry Lanscombe, he had his own doubts. Death had come too swiftly, too sharply on the nail. If the man had taken his own life, why now? If it had been a careless accident, why at this point in time? If neither of these was an explanation, then Nemesis had come to Larry Lanscombe in human form and with fearful speed . . .

And perhaps it was he, Kemp, who had been the unwitting instigator, who had triggered off somehow, somewhere, a hidden force . . . He tried to shake such thoughts from him as he walked back to his car through the grey streets, but instinct made him keep glancing over his shoulder as if he might catch out of the corner of his eye the flare of a scarlet skirt.

FIFTEEN

BY THE TIME Kemp had driven back to his office he was in a state of frustrated irritability, the kind that builds up from self-doubt, indecision and fatigue, not unmixed with guilt. He was ready to vent it on the nearest target to justify his attention.

Nick Stoddart was unlucky enough to present himself as such. He had breezed into Kemp's room, shoulders thrust forward like a charging bull, his head nodding up and down as if to affirm whatever devious scheme lay within, his face carefully arranged in the manner of one who bears good news for himself, discomfort to his enemies.

'Just been up to Careys,' he said, perching on the end of Kemp's desk, 'thought you ought to be the first to know. They've offered me a job as head of their litigation department.'

'I don't give a damn if they've offered you the job of Lord Chancellor,' Kemp snapped. 'Sit down, Nick. There.' He pointed to the chair opposite to his own. 'I've got a thing or two to say to you.'

'Pity you're taking it badly, old boy...' Stoddart began, but he caught the look in Kemp's eye, slid off the desk and sat down. 'Didn't expect you'd be pleased.'

'I bloody well am pleased. Careys can have you any time. Now we've got that little matter settled, let's get back to something else. Higgs Electric, twenty years ago. I want the facts, all of them, and this time I want the truth.'

Stoddart gave a snicker of a laugh. 'Not that old stuff again. Come off it, Lennox, you're just cross because I've stolen a march on you.'

'Cross I may be, but that's not the reason. You can take your undoubted talents wherever you like, but not before you've told me everything I want to know about that episode in your past.' Kemp was trying to keep cool, and not allow his dislike of the man to colour his judgement. Essential now to get at the truth . . .

'You're just trying to stop me leaving! I think that's a pretty poor show, Lennox, playing dog-in-the-manger. You want to take this thing up simply to spoil my chances.'

'It was you who started it, remember? And in more ways than one. If you sow dragons' teeth you have to live with the strife that follows.' Kemp was wearied by Stoddart's attitude—small-minded, like his head. Should he say, a man has died? The connection was as yet too tenuous. He would have to try the soft approach.

'Look here, Nick, I only want to know more about the Higgs affair for my own personal reasons. It's important to me whether Charles Copeland is telling the truth. His version is different from yours.'

That got through to him. Stoddart leant forward.

'What's the little bastard been saying?'

Kemp told him, baldly.

By the time he'd finished the other man's face was grim. It was also patchily brick-red.

'He says I took money as well as him?'

Kemp nodded.

'It's his word against mine.' It was like an echo of Charley's complaint. 'Well, I did not. I'll not say I wasn't tempted, but I didn't take any money. 'Nick Stoddart's eyes were deadly serious, no longer belligerent. 'You have to believe that, Lennox.'

'You told me, Nick, that you caught Charley out. That's exactly what you said. It wasn't like that, was it?'

Stoddart got up, pushed his hands into his pockets and walked across to the window where he stood, staring out. He did not turn round as he answered.

'If I tell you what really happened, twenty years ago, will you give me your promise that it will go no further?'

Kemp sighed; he would have to seek, as lawyers do, the perfect form of words, encapsulating reassurance on the one hand and cover for every eventuality on the other. Tie the parcel up tight but with one loose string . . .

He chose his words with care.

'If, when you have told me the facts and the truth about your part, I decide that nobody has been harmed, or will be harmed, by such divulgence, then I give you my word I will hold what you have told me in confidence, and nothing we say in this room now will be repeated outside it. If I find you have lied to me—as you've obviously already done—I shall be under no obligation to respect that confidence.'

Even Stoddart's head had remained still while he listened. He's noting each word, thought Kemp grimly, I wonder if he's aware of the full implications?

Stoddart turned suddenly, and returned to his seat as though he had come to a decision, and wished to give the impression the decision had been his own and not arrived at under pressure.

'I'll trust you, Lennox,' he began, as one conferring a favour, 'and tell you the facts as I know them, because it looks like Charles is trying to wriggle out of his part in it by putting the blame on me, and I won't stand for it . . .'

Kemp smiled slightly.

'Never mind having a go at Charley again. You want to square things with me before you go on to Careys, and I'm giving you the chance to do just that.' Kemp decided it was time to slow things down, allow a breathing space . . . 'Coffee, Nick?'

'Yes, thanks. Black.'

Kemp rang for Elvira to bring it, Nick started talking about his early days, and the friendship which had arisen between the two youths in Gillorns' office. When the tray of cups was brought he and Kemp appeared to be chatting amicably about the past.

Never thought I'd see those two getting on so well, thought Elvira as she withdrew, I wonder what Mr Kemp's up to? She recalled an old phrase of his from the Walthamstow days: 'Softly, softly, catchee monkey'... He'd been good at that.

As if naturally out of the conversation, Stoddart got to the nub.

'It was through my father I met Major Bulett. He'd been a friend of my dad's in the Territorials—really only a passing acquaintance I subsequently found out. Anyway, through my father's influence I had the entry to this London club. Great place to have drinks when the pubs were shut, and I'd begun taking Charley there after work. He was easily impressed, Charley, in those days...'

In essence, you were showing-off, thought Kemp, but knew better than to say so.

'Major Bulett was quite a character, a military man and well-bred. I didn't twig at first just why he took us up, Charles and me. But later... well, he'd heard from my father where we both worked... It was obvious afterwards, of course. We'd had that case for Edmonton Mutual in for months. It wasn't important, small stuff...'

Kemp waited.

Stoddart drank his coffee, stretched his legs, and with them his memories of another age, another time, removed from the present by two decades of changing fashions, politics and ethics.

'It was the 'sixties, you must remember...' Like others had done, and were continuing to do, he was using that era as an excuse, ignoring the fact that Kemp too had lived through, and beyond, it. 'We were young and I suppose we were influenced by the new freedoms, youth and all that. A bit anti-establishment, eh?' Stoddart paused and looked to Kemp for some measure of empathy, but was ill-rewarded.

Whatever Kemp's own recollections or opinions were of those swinging times, he was not putting them up for barter.

'I see,' was his only comment as he went on staring at Stoddart, his eyes vacant, his expression receptive, no more.

'At first, all that Major Bulett wanted was information,' said Stoddart, 'what the other side was alleging against Higgs, that kind of thing. In short, what was holding up payment of the claim. He had a responsibility, he said, towards the firm of which he was the general manager at the time of the fire, and he was a bit narked, as he put it, by the case having to go to Court at all.'

It wasn't hard for Kemp to see the picture, two young men being patronized in a clubby atmosphere of convivial drinks and smokes.

Nick Stoddart took a deep breath. 'I was feeling a bit browned-off with Gillorns at the time,' he said. 'They were treating me like a bloody stamp-licker. Well, that was all right for Charley—that was his job—but not for me. So I'm afraid I gave out rather more than I should. You understand?'

Kemp did, only too well. The tendency of the young, particularly the disgruntled young, is for self-aggrandisement, the temptation to show themselves as more at the centre of things than they really are. It was a common enough affliction.

'But when it came to the crunch—' now Stoddart was speaking with studied earnestness—'when the Major—and this was a week or two later—actually offered us money to lose certain documents, to, as it were, twist the evidence even before it got to Court, well, then, by Jove, I backed out . . .'

And hurrah for you, thought Kemp sardonically, God bless the public school spirit!

'I really didn't need the money, anyway,' said Stoddart, disarmingly, 'but Charley certainly did. He was desperate to get married.'

'And you encouraged him to take this bribe?'

Nick Stoddart was intelligent enough to let the remark pass without comment.

'Afterwards, I supposed he'd taken it. Well, I knew he had. He'd been responsible for getting the paperwork in order, having the stuff typed and checked. By the time I went to Court with Counsel it was obvious half the case for the insurers was missing... You see, I was right, Lennox—' he leaned eagerly forward across the desk, anxious that his point should be made—'when I told you I'd caught Charley out taking a bribe. He had taken it...'

'But a bribe you had prior knowledge of. Something of which you should have apprised your superiors.' Kemp could not keep distaste from his voice.

'How could I give Charles away? He'd been my friend. I knew his circumstances... Would you have told on him?' Nick managed to sound righteously indignant.

'This isn't the time to discuss the ethics of the situation,' Kemp relied coldly, wondering if the man was going to bring up that old chestnut, do you betray your country or your friend? 'Let's stick to the facts, shall we?'

He proceeded to question Stoddart closely about the case itself without giving away the details he had already assimilated from the old papers. He had to grant that the litigation lawyer was almost word-perfect, he had a fine memory and now, when forced to use it to save his own skin, his answers corresponded accurately with everything Kemp had discovered for himself. There were also new features brought up which Kemp stacked away in his own mind to sort out later as to their relevance.

'And that's all I can remember about the blasted case... Wish I'd never heard of either Major Bulett or Higgs Electric,' Stoddart ended bleakly.

'You've done very well, Nick,' Kemp complimented him.

Stoddart eyed him with suspicion.

'Some of those questions... You know something, don't you?'

'I've looked up the file.'

'You mean it was never thrown out? Bloody hell!'

'Sometimes the old man's habit of housekeeping pays off, Nick, despite adding to the clutter of Clements Inn.'

'But why'd you go to all that bother? You're prepared to overlook what Charles did. Look, I'm sorry I ever brought it up... I admit now it was spite. Just couldn't stand that smug pi-face of his... You're not going to use that file, are you?' he added apprehensively.

'I gave you my word, Nick. And if it's any comfort to you, there's nothing there which contradicts anything you've told me.'

'Thank God for that.' Stoddart paused. 'You do rather go into things, Lennox, I'll say that for you.'

'I believe in being thorough, if that's what you mean. Now you've given me the facts, I'd like you to join me in a little theorizing. At the time the Major approached you and Charley with the offer of money, what did you actually think—apart from having scruples?'

Nick answered promptly. 'That Major Bulett was going to a lot of trouble, chucking away a fair amount of cash, and taking a big risk...'

'Why should he do that?'

Stoddart had relaxed, and was letting his experience and his intellect work for him. 'I did wonder about that at the time... He said he hadn't wanted the matter to go to litigation at all. He'd have taken the insurers' first offer, but the big company, of which Higgs was a mere offshoot, wouldn't accept.'

'They were a household name?'

'Exactly, and had the necessary clout.'

'But the Major couldn't, or wouldn't, allow any suspicion of negligence to fall on Higgs Electric?'

'That's what I thought. After all, it was his job that was at stake—that must have mattered at first, for from what I could gather, he was on his beam ends... Later, things changed for the better.'

'He took a hell of a risk,' Kemp interrupted, 'offering a bribe to employees in a firm of solicitors. What if you had gone straight to your principal?'

'Major Bulett would have laughed it off. Said it was all a joke... Or a test of our integrity. And he'd have got away with it. He was that kind of man.'

'What happened to him?'

'For God's sake, Lennox, I couldn't have cared less. I certainly never wanted to set eyes on him again.'

'But you must have had some curiosity,' Kemp persisted. 'Think about it.'

'Well, I never went back to that club to find out, if that's what you're getting at. I wanted to keep right out of the whole nasty business.' Nick was becoming self-righteous again.

'I'm sure you did,' Kemp observed ironically, 'but you must have heard something more about him. It would only be natural for you to inquire.'

'I think my father did tell me later on that Major Bulett had gone to the States,' said Stoddart reluctantly.

Kemp raised his eyebrows. 'The man appears to have had means.'

'Oh, he had plenty of money,' said Nick surprisingly. 'Father said it had come suddenly by way of inheritance. A family trust of long standing was finally wound up. He hadn't always had it, otherwise he wouldn't have been working in an outfit like Higgs.'

'So he could well afford to bribe a couple of susceptible young law clerks...'

Nick Stoddart decided to let the remark pass without comment, taking the words, though barbed, as mere aside.

Anyway, Kemp was pursuing his own line of thought. 'Was there any particular name mentioned either in the missing correspondence, or in the parts of the investigators' report that got left out? I presume they were destroyed?'

Stoddart moved uneasily.

'Letters were certainly removed, and certain bits of the report had been excised. They didn't amount to much—a few paragraphs here and there, that kind of thing.' Now that he had got his second wind, Stoddart was all set to minimize the whole affair. 'Let's face it, Lennox, it was no big deal. All the insurers wanted was to knock off a few thousands for negligence on the part of Higgs themselves—if they could prove it. They never expected to find themselves in Court. It was only the big company who dug their toes in, thinking of their good name, I suppose, even if Higgs was only a subsidiary of theirs. And the last thing Bulett wanted was a legal battle.'

'H'm. He was hiding something, that's for sure. I wonder what the hell it was...'

'Well, he didn't set the place on fire for the insurance moneys, I can tell you that. He wouldn't have gained a penny. And in all the documentation I saw there'd never been any allegations that the fire was started deliberately. It was fully accepted from the outset that it was accidental.'

Kemp decided it was time to stop theorizing and get back to the nuts and bolts of legal procedure, the way in which such cases are run.

'Discovery, Nick?' Kemp said it quietly.

Stoddart considered how far he could afford to go. 'A rush job, old boy. Remember, they were Higgs's solicitors, not the company's... They sent a green lad. Perhaps the Major had been busy there too. The copy correspondence and their investigators' report tallied with ours. That's all I'm prepared to say...'

Kemp let it pass. He had other things on his mind.

'There was a fatality in that fire.'

Stoddart looked genuinely surprised. 'Was there? Oh Lor', I'd forgotten. But it had nothing to do with the case.

We only had to deal with the insurance claim on the premises.'

'Did you ever give it a thought?'

'Why on earth should I? It would have been dealt with somewhere else. I did read about it, of course, in the fire chief's report right at the beginning of the file but it seemed to have been cleared up, inquest and all. Some typist or other who was working late. Not much reward, that, for diligence.'

'Let's get back to the question I asked before, Nick. You admit you read all the papers, including the missing letters and the parts of the report which didn't come up in Court, was there any name mentioned? What about this question of faulty wiring?'

Stoddart was screwing his eyes up in an effort to remember. At least that's what he appeared to be doing, and Kemp didn't consider acting to be Nick's strong point—judging by what he had said, he left that to the other branch of the profession.

'I honestly can't recall any names,' he said at length, 'if indeed there were any mentioned. That wiring now...the firemen believed the fire started in the storeroom and spread from there to the offices above, and the investigation seemed to confirm they were right. There were some rather dodgy bits of wire strung across the place in a rather amateurish fashion—possibly for lighting on the work benches, and the storeman making cups of tea...'

'And that was where the Edmonton Mutual alleged there had been negligence?'

Stoddart nodded.

'Does the name Lawrence, or Larry, Lanscombe mean anything to you?' asked Kemp.

'Not a thing. Who's he?'

'He was the storeman, and supposed to be a dab hand with electrical jobs.'

'That figures. From what I gathered the place was run on a tight budget, the company weren't wasting any money on it. This Lanscombe chap probably did all the maintenance, ran the stores and mended vacuum-cleaners in his spare time—if any. The Major believed in getting his work-force to toe the line.'

'Then why should he go to such lengths to protect the storeman if he'd been to blame for the fire starting?'

'Search me. As I told you, the Major hadn't wanted the case to get as far as a courtroom. All he'd been interested in was getting a quick settlement. He certainly wasn't the sort to protect anyone, least of all one of his menials. He'd have fired him on the spot, and let him take the consequences. He was Bulett by name and Bully by nature from what I saw of him. Incidentally, his first name was Gerald—call me Gerry, he used to say.'

You found him affable enough at that club, thought Kemp, but he changed the subject abruptly.

'Charles says he told his wife about the money—and the circumstances.'

'Well, he had to, hadn't he? He needed her.'

'To get married, you mean?' said Kemp stupidly.

'No, you chump—' Stoddart had certainly perked up—'to do the typing. Didn't you spot her reference on the letters? RF—that was old Fenimore who was half-asleep most of the time—stroke DL. Dorothea Lingard, as she was then...' Nick stopped, his eyes taking on a reflective look. 'That was a real turn-up for the book. Not Charley taking the money but our demure little Dottie going along with it. Made it a lot easier, of course; any other typist in the office might have noticed the missing bits, and I'll say this for our Dorothea, she was bright...'

'She wanted to get married?' Kemp hazarded.

'Sure she did, but she was supposed to have such high principles. I couldn't understand it at the time. Still don't.'

'Did you ever take her out?' asked Kemp.

'Once or twice,' said Stoddart warily. 'Never got to first base. Anyway she soon latched on to Charley, and obviously he had better luck.'

Nick's tone was scathing but there was underlying resentment in it also. Perhaps that early friendship had foundered on other rocks than the Higgs affair, thought Kemp. He knew Stoddart had had an unhappy marriage, ending in a particularly vituperative divorce; it looked as if his denunciation of Charles Copeland had sprung from a deeper motive than sheer spite.

Stoddart was beginning to show signs of restlessness, and Kemp glanced at his watch. Had it all been a waste of time, this digging up of old sins, these revelations of grubby practices twenty years ago, tainted with the self-interest of all concerned? What did they add up to but small misdeeds and youthful indiscretion?

He got to his feet, and said, wearily: 'I think you've been honest with me, Nick, to the best of your knowledge, and I'll stick to my part of our bargain, with of course the provisos already made. And I shall not put anything in the way of your leaving us.'

'Thank goodness for that!' Nick Stoddart rose too, glad now to be out of the penitent's chair. 'I haven't lied to you, Lennox, and as for anyone having been harmed in this matter, there's been no evidence of it these twenty years. What possible harm could there be to anyone now?'

'You tried to harm Charles,' Kemp reminded him sternly, 'and you have to take responsibility for that.'

Stoddart hesitated. 'If you want me to—' he brought the words out after a struggle with himself—'I'll apologize to him before I leave.'

'It would be a kindly gesture, Nick, but make it casual—no recriminations, please.'

SIXTEEN

GERALD BULETT ENTERED the apartment rubbing his hands, partly from cold for it was one o'clock in the morning and frosty outside, but also as an expression of self-congratulation. He'd had a busy day in the City followed by late dinner and a visit to a night club in celebration of the deal successfully concluded.

He was surprised to find her still up, sprawled in the armchair with a drink in her hand. He went over and kissed her.

'Well, Quin, I've brought Cavendish and his lot right up to the trough. He'll sign that contract tomorrow.'

'Not before time.' She scarcely turned her head, and her tone was surly. The frost had obviously come into the room with him. 'If you'd let me do the talking, he'd have signed it a week ago. You're getting soft in the head, Gerry, you're losing your punch.'

She was in a bad mood, a grudging mood. No point in arguing with her. He poured himself a drink and threw himself on the sofa. She never missed an opportunity to take him down a peg. All right, if it was the way she wanted, then two could play that game. Feeling euphoric himself, he searched for a way to get even.

She had partly undressed down to her black satin slip over the scarlet swinging skirt which he hated. The dark leather jacket she wore with it lay on the floor at her feet.

'I don't like you in that outfit. Makes you look like a tart.'

She swung her legs down from the chair and pushed past him to the drinks cabinet, letting the red skirt trail over his glass as she went by.

'Boloney,' she said, splashing whisky into her tumbler, 'It's smart to be common in London these days. East End, West End, what's the difference? Looked good, it did, this outfit—down the Hertford High Road.'

That'll take the swagger out of him, she thought, coming in here like a conquering hero...

Her words had the desired effect.

'What the devil?' He was on his feet, glaring at her. 'Where the hell have you been?'

'Oh, out and about, you know... Here and there...' She put on the voice of a stylish career girl she'd recently seen on a television car advertisement. When she'd seen it she'd thought, savagely: With my wits and that creature's looks twenty years back, I'd have got a seat on the board of directors... Shallow she might be but she'd always known her own worth.

Bulett took her by the shoulder and swung her round, her drink spattering the flowered cretonne of the chair-cover. 'I want to know what the hell you've been up to!'

She wriggled free, and walked calmly back to her chair.

'You come right over here, honey, and I'll tell you.'

There was a little table between them, a fragile piece with a pie-crust top. She put her drink down on it, searched the pocket of her scarlet skirt for a scrap of a hankie, and dried the spilled liquor from her fingers. The gold bracelets up her arms jangled; they could have been imitation the way she wore them but he knew they were gold. Like that other one she'd worn... He wasn't going to think about that...

'Stop acting like a bull in a china shop,' she said. 'Nervous, are we?'

He walked across and took the other chair, setting down his whisky tumbler with a thump that made the table ring.

'What's all this about the Hertford High Road?' he said, but more quietly now.

'I went and had a look at the old place.'

'Whatever for, Quin?' He was determined to control his temper; losing it always lost him the match with her.

'For auld lang syne, my dear, for auld lang syne...' she sang in the high, cracked voice he loathed. But she broke off, and her face was serious, the black eyes narrowed and cunning. 'I tell you this, Gerry, it was as well I went there.'

'What do you mean?'

'I wasn't the only one snooping around down Alma Street.'

He drew in his breath sharply. 'You went to Alma Street?'

'Yep. Right to the door, of fifty-four. Ain't gonna need this house no longer, ain't gonna need this house no more...'

'Stop that damned singing, you bitch!' He closed his eyes briefly against the uselessness of words. 'Just tell me what happened. This is too serious for your cabaret turn.'

'You can say that again. Yeah, it's serious. And it would've been a lot worse if your Queenie hadn't been on the spot.' Now she was back to her normal voice, the one she used for business, a low, not unattractive contralto which could be both incisive and persuasive, and which had proved one of her greatest assets.

He listened to it now, at first with disbelief, and then with growing horror as, without emotion, she told him not only about Alma Street, but Balaclava Street as well.

He'd closed his eyes before she'd come to the end. It was more than he could bear. If he opened them he might see again that sordid little house at 43 Balaclava Street... Ye gods, he could still remember the number! That awful peeling linoleum down the passage to the kitchen where Mrs Lanscombe sat like a fat toad, her beady eyes on the alert.

Larry had shuffled him into the parlour, and slumped down himself on the old-fashioned horsehair settee, pale, miserable and frightened out of his wits.

'I was working late, sir. I swear I never heard nothing...'

'Don't you believe him,' Queenie had hissed on the telephone, 'he was there all right, and I bet he heard everything. Get rid of him. I know Larry, he'll take money. Just keep him out of things...'

Bulett couldn't remember what else she'd told him about that night. He'd shut the memory out for so long...

He'd played the avuncular figure to the shaking Larry, admonishing but understanding.

'So you'd fixed up that little corner for yourself with an electric stove, and a kettle to make tea? Against fire regulations, that was, my boy... Tea-making facilities were upstairs in the office. Bad show if this got out. And it was your own wiring? Never inspected by the Electricity Board? That wouldn't go down well in the investigation report.'

Larry had been easy, shivering in his shoes, a scared rabbit.

'Better keep it dark about you working late. The fire was an accident—let's not complicate matters...'

And to Mrs Lanscombe Bulett had been the company commander, speaking in an incisive baritone: 'Don't worry, I'll see your lad doesn't get into trouble. Must look after my men, you know...'

Later, just in case Larry had second thoughts, money had passed.

Now, at the end of a day which should have brought him jubilation, Major Bulett put his head in his hands, and groaned.

SEVENTEEN

IT WAS SOME DAYS before Kemp could bring himself to call on Mr McIlvey. It was true what he'd told the men in the Inkerman Arms—he had no wish to cause the old man any further distress. But curiosity was a ravening beast where Kemp was concerned, and would give him no peace until he'd driven it back into its lair.

He found the McIlveys' flat easily enough, just in from the street. The woman who came to the door had a lined face and eyes that had seen adversity, but the corners of her mouth had a perky upturn as if she'd laughed at most of it.

'Mr Kemp? Oh yes, he told me about you. He's in there by the fire, out of the chill,' she said as she stood to one side in the little hall, clutching a rubber-shod stick in one gnarled hand. Kemp was reassured on two counts: that she at least bore him no malice, and that she had a care for her husband.

The small figure of Mr McIlvey was almost hidden in the depths of an armchair, but he struggled to his feet.

'Am I glad to see you, Mr Kemp! Dear, dear, what a sad business it's been.'

'I'll get the tea.' Mrs McIlvey didn't waste words. 'You get back in that chair, Ted.'

The old man subsided into a nest of cushions and rugs.

'Got a touch of the cold, like,' he said apologetically, 'The missus, she worries . . . Sit yerself down, Mr Kemp.'

It was a small room, crammed with ornaments. Kemp drew up a chair in front of the fire, which was going to be very hot. He slipped off his jacket.

'Doctor said I'd not to go out. So the police came here. Ye'll have seen them too?'

Kemp nodded. 'They had my card, picked it up at the house.'

The old man went into a lengthy explanation, punctuated by fits of coughing. Kemp poured him a small glass of linctus from a bottle on the sideboard. 'It's my chest,' said Mr McIlvey, patting it. 'Gets me in the wintertime. Where'd I get to?'

'You'd gone round to his house when he came home from work that evening—the evening of the day I met you.'

'Seen him go past, like he allus does. Waited a bit. Let the man get his supper, the missus says, so I did. Be around seven when I got there. He was just finishing his meal, but he was off to the darts, he said, so he'd no time to stop. I talked to him while he washed up the dishes. Very tidy, Larry, allus had been ... That sergeant, now, the one that came here, he says that was Larry's last meal. They'd know that from the stomach contents, wouldn't they?'

Kemp nodded. He could see that Mr McIlvey was making an effort to be practical, using words he'd heard.

'Pork pie, chips and peas. I seen that's what it was before he cleared the table, and that's what I told the police.'

'What did Mr Lanscombe say when you told him about me?'

'Well, he didn't take a lot of notice at first, like, when I just said I'd met a man in the pub lunch-time. He knew me, I reckon, allus ready for a chat with strangers ...' The old man looked across at Kemp as if he would understand the frailty.

'But when you mentioned the fire at Higgs?' Kemp prompted softly.

'He were at the sink with his back to me, and he turned round ever so sharp like. What's that bein' raked up for, he said. Well, I said, I dunno, perhaps you was just interested in fires ... Like for an insurance company, you being a lawyer... I could see Larry was upset. He dropped the dish-cloth on the floor, and I picked it up for him. I told him straight that you'd not mentioned his name. It were one of the others said he'd been the storeman at Higgs...'

He was a garrulous man, Mr McIlvey, thought Kemp sadly, he must have told Larry Lanscombe about their sub-sequent chat over drinks. It would be on his conscience, but perhaps not lying so heavily as it was on Kemp's.

'You don't think me telling him about you had anything to do with... what he did?' The bleared eyes looking anx-iously at Kemp were almost pleading.

Kemp shook his head. 'I don't see how it could,' he said, with more conviction than he felt. 'My name would mean nothing to him. You gave him my card?'

'I put it down on the table. He only gave it a glance, said he'd have to be off to the pub by half-seven. He fair bus-tled me out... Weren't time really to say more, and any-way I could see he'd got himself into a mood.'

'What sort of mood?'

'Restless, like. Didn't want to talk. Well, he wouldn't, would he, being in a hurry as he was.' Mr McIlvey sank back into his chair, and dabbed at his eyes. 'When we heard next morning... It was his neighbour told us, she's friendly with Grace, she came round right away. She said she wasn't sur-prised at what he'd done, she'd seen him get right de-pressed at times...'

Grace McIlvey herself heard the words as she wheeled in a squeaky trolley. Kemp jumped up to help her with the cups, and the teapot, saw a large sponge-cake and a plate of toast.

'This is very kind of you. You shouldn't have gone to the trouble...'

'No trouble. It's for him—and you too if you've a mind to it. Yes, Larry got depressed. All the years I've known him he'd have these fits of it. Morose, that's how he'd get. What a wasted life!'

As she expertly, despite arthritic hands and hip, dispensed tea, and toast, and cut the cake in fair slices, Kemp heard from her all she knew of Larry Lanscombe's history. And a melancholy tale it proved to be.

'It was that fire,' she ended decisively. 'Mrs Lanscombe said Larry was never the same after it. Should have been the making of him, that money he got, and them buying the house...'

'Where do you think the money came from, Mrs McIlvey?'

'He told his mother it was part of the insurance. Might've fooled her, didn't fool me. The firm would get that, why'd they pay out anything to an employee? Later the word got round his mates that it was redundancy... And that was a lie, 'cos that didn't come in till a couple of years later. I know all about that because Ted was one of the first to get it when he lost his job at the gas works... And that was only a hundred or so, and he'd been there since he left school.' Mrs McIlvey shook her head. 'No, where the money came from was a mystery... And it never made Larry happy, though it pleased his ma to get the house.'

Grace McIlvey evidently had a lively, practical mind, not blunted by disuse or dimmed by the passing of the years.

'How old would Larry be at the time of the fire?'

'He'd be twenty-two or -three when we came to live next door to them, and the fire'd been the previous year. He'd just started his job at the timber-yard—and that was a bit of a come down... But he'd given up going to the tech for his City and Guilds like he should've done. Mrs Lanscombe told me that before the fire at Higgs he'd been up there most nights at his classes, she said...'

There was a chuckle from the armchair.

'That's what he told his ma. The rumour was that Larry was out most nights with the girls.'

'That's as maybe. We mustn't speak ill...'

'Did he bring any of these girls home?'

'Lawks, no! His mother was a right old Mrs Grundy, and stuck-up, too. No girl from round here would be good enough for her Larry.'

'He were a handsome lad,' put in Mr McIlvey, 'I reckon he had girls falling all over him in them days.'

'Well, he never had them to the house. More cake, Mr Kemp? It's only shop-bought. My fingers can't cope with the mixing...'

She made a sudden excited movement. 'I tell a lie,' she exclaimed. 'There was a girl. Mrs Lanscombe told me years later, when she'd got more friendly, like, and was a bit sentimental. She said Larry'd brought a girl to tea once or twice—and that would be before the fire, the way she spoke. She was a well-brought-up young woman, and got good manners—well, she'd need to have if Mrs Lanscombe approved of her. But that's the only one she ever spoke about.'

'She didn't mention the girl's name?'

Grace McIlvey let out a sigh. 'It's so long ago... She might have, but it's gone from me. Come to think of it, it was a pretty name... No, it's gone. Why'd you ask, Mr Kemp?'

'I don't know, Mrs McIlvey. I'm still trying to put together a clear picture of Larry as he was.'

'It'll be a terrible thing if they find he took his own life.' Grace was not the weeping kind, but her sorrow showed in her voice. 'But there's no doubt he was lonely after his mother died. It weren't natural, him on his own in that house. I blame the whisky, myself.'

'The landlord at the Inkerman Arms says Larry wasn't a great drinker,' Kemp observed.

'Little they knew,' said Mrs McIlvey, shaking her head slowly from side to side. 'But I've been in there late at night when I'd take back his washing, and he'd have that whisky bottle out. When he got depressed, he'd drink at home. And he'd take those pills the doctors kept giving him—for the depression, they said.'

'What the policeman told me when he came, Mr Kemp—' the old man spoke haltingly—'was that the bottle was empty, and so was the wee carton of capsules he'd had from the doctor. Mebbe he got hisself into such a state he didn't know what he was doing when he turned on the gas...'

'It could well have happened like that,' said Kemp, with more hope than he felt, as he put on his jacket, and said goodbye to Mr McIlvey.

The old couple had been saddened by the death, and by their own doubts as to its cause, even though they had not seen so much of Larry Lanscombe in the last few years, since Grace had had to give up going to his house—as she put it—to do a few chores for a bachelor man.

'We did what we could,' she said as she showed Kemp to the door, 'but Larry'd shut himself off from people. Never went out except to his work, and down to the pub for the darts. Depression's a fearful thing if you're alone, and at his age... That policeman who came, he was nice... Said it could have been an accident, that he got in a stupor with the drink and those damned pills and didn't get the gas lit properly...' She shuddered. 'There ought to be a law against them kind of pills.' Then in a softer tone: 'But, Ted and me, we've been lucky, never needing stuff like that. We've had our ups and downs, and sometimes it's been real hard, but you got to keep going, haven't you?'

IT WOULD BE SOME COMFORT to them if it was found to have been an unfortunate accident, thought Kemp as he walked back up Alma Street. He glanced across at the mercilessly contemporary façade of bright, blank, glazed brick where No. 54 had once stood, and wondered.

But whether the verdict be misadventure or suicide, it wasn't going to let him off the hook. Why did it happen on that particular night? Kemp took out one of his business cards; his own name of course would have meant nothing to

Lanscombe, but in the corner were the words 'Gillorns, Solicitors'... Would a mere storeman at the time have been conversant with the name of the legal firm who dealt with the matter of Higgs Electric and the Edmonton Mutual, and would he have cause to remember it after all these years? The card between Kemp's fingers seemed to stare back at him with reproach.

The last time he'd been down these grey streets he had left undone things which he ought to have done, and now he was haunted by the possibility that the lapse had cost a life. He must not make the same error again, so he directed his feet towards the police station.

Detective-Inspector Inskip was out but Sergeant Lucas gave Kemp all the information that was available.

'Could have been an accident, I suppose,' he said, pursing his lips, 'the post-mortem showed a stomach full of whisky and pills, though it was the gas that finished him off.'

'Wasn't that overdoing it a bit,' said Kemp, 'drink, drugs *and* the gas oven?'

'A determined suicide would go the whole hog,' said Lucas in the tone of one who had seen it all, 'but it's up to the Coroner. A verdict of misadventure's kinder to them that's left, though it's never brought anyone back from the dead.' Lucas seemed to have a peculiarly mordant sense of humour but Kemp's thoughts were, for the moment, disengaged. I've had this kind of thing running in my mind recently—where was it now? Oh yes, that friend of Mrs Copeland's... I'll be lurching into platitudes next if I don't watch out, he told himself, getting back briskly to the subject on hand.

'Those pills Mr Lanscombe was taking, were they on prescription?'

'All above board. He had them through his local GP, Dr Mallory's his name, local man, runs a good practice, overworked like most of them round here. Said he hadn't seen

Lanscombe for a month or so but he did have bouts of depression, and the prescription was regular enough. Never enough for suicide, though, unless he hoarded them, and there was only the one carton found and Dr Mallory says that wasn't enough to do any harm. Lanscombe's depression wasn't serious, according to the doc, at least not medically speaking, just his age, lack of contact with people—loneliness, I suppose...'

'Makes him sound like an ageing spinster lady.'

Lucas hooted with laughter. 'Spinster ladies growing old at forty-five? Not around here they don't. They're down at the Bingo hall with a Guinness at their elbow!'

'What was Lanscombe like at work?'

'Got on well with his mates, and the bosses too, for that matter. A good worker, they said, conscientious, never late, but a bit of a loner, and lacked initiative. Skilful with his hands, should have gone further than he did.'

'The inspector got any ideas as to why this lone depressive should take his own life when he did—if he did?' Kemp asked casually.

Lucas moved his shoulders. 'Nope. Just the depression.'

'Hit him a bit sudden, didn't it? He'd just won a match for the darts team.'

'I heard about that. One of his mates was in with the Inspector, telling the tale. Seems he was the last person to see Mr Lanscombe that night, left him at the corner of his street.'

'I suppose they'd done a spot of celebrating before leaving the pub. Lanscombe might have been half seas over before he got to the whisky...' Kemp was ruminating. 'Too much to drink only depressed him, so he got out the pills. What on earth made him turn on the oven?'

'You working on the accident theory?' Sergeant Lucas seemed ready to oblige. 'Well, he was found on the floor beside the open oven door. It's an old-fashioned low stove, and he'd have to stoop to light the burners at the back.

Funny thing, he did have one of these oven gloves on his hand...'

'So he could have stooped and fallen, having already turned on the tap but not lit the burners? Anything in the oven?'

'A dish with a few chips left over from his supper. You could be right about an accident... But I don't think there were any marks of a fall, looked more like he just laid himself down. So you pays your money and takes your pick, eh?'

'No suggestion then of foul play?'

Sergeant Lucas had been loquacious up till now. He cocked an eye at Kemp.

'Not that we found. Do you always do this?'

'What?'

'Show such an interest. I understand from Inspector Inskip that you didn't actually know this Mr Lanscombe.'

'True, but I am interested in how he came to die.'

'Seems clear enough to me. You one of these lawyers that'll make a murder out of a molehill?'

Kemp winced, as much at the mixed metaphor as at the accusation.

'I certainly wouldn't want to set off a murder inquiry,' he said, mildly and meaning every word, 'but we lawyers have to leave no stone unturned, explore every avenue, follow whatever scent...' He decided he'd thrown enough clichés around to disguise his intentions. 'I only wondered if the neighbours of Mr Lanscombe had seen or heard anything unusual that night.'

'Nope. It's quiet as a grave down there at night—if you'll pardon the expression—and this was no exception. His light was on late, that was noticed by a neighbour, but it wasn't unusual, for he'd sit up late with the whisky when he couldn't sleep. Of course we know that light was on all night but there's no passers-by down there after the pubs shut—

and not many after. It's a dead end—there I go again!' Lucas had quite a sense of humour.

And a very dead end it was for Larry Lanscombe, thought Kemp wryly as he left the station.

Drawn there by invisible threads of conscience and curiosity, he walked once again down to the railway end of Balaclava Street. The little terrace itself looked as if it was not long for this world, cowering under the threat of the great yellow bulldozers already at work in the cleared hinterland behind it. They'd forged a path for themselves beside the embankment and into the next street where once he supposed there must have been a narrow alley leading to the back yards. He strolled down it, kicking up the dust; the surface was covered by the giant caterpillar tracks, but anyone could have lurked there, even a car late at night ...

He went back and stopped outside No. 43. There was no milk bottle on the step today, and the laburnum looked sadder than ever. No one would tend that rockery any more, and the brave paint on the woodwork would soon fade, and peel off in the summer sun. By then the house would be boarded up, ready to be eaten by the Council. Sergeant Lucas had told him Larry Lanscombe seemed to have no folks, so Kemp guessed that, in time, statutory notices would reach the plaintive little columns of newspapers where lawyers seek long-lost kin, and if none came forward, the wretched estate would land *in bona vacantia* before falling at last into the gently-smiling crocodile jaws of the Crown.

So much for the aspirations of the strict Methodist woman who'd lived there with her son, for whom life had come to mean nothing more than a menial task, a game of darts, and a whisky bottle at the days' end ...

I must stop coming here, Kemp thought gloomily, the place exhales depression like the whirling detritus being kicked up by those infernal earth-movers.

Time I got back to life, and some rational thinking.

EIGHTEEN

WHEN GERALD BULETT came into the apartment that February afternoon he thought the whole interior looked like a great white crystal bowl. It's just the brilliance of sudden spring sunshine, he told himself, trying to be sensible and not give way to such fancies. He'd been seeing things differently since she'd talked to him about Alma Street, and this had altered even his vision, normally straightforward, taking in only the material aspects of rooms and furniture, ceilings and carpets, as an ordinary man would—not imagining them set in a crystal bowl . . .

Yet the notion persisted, and she, sitting at the black marble table, white elbows reflected on its surface, fingers entwined, her face in shadow, was the spider in the centre of a spangled web . . . The sun's rays struck horizontal bars through the half-draped windows, and splintered on the decanters and glasses of the drinks cabinet. He felt like brushing away the golden flecks that danced along the dusty beams as if they were in fact wispy strands of cobweb . . .

He was not an imaginative man but now a key seemed to have been turned in a little-used part of his brain, releasing perceptions he couldn't cope with and bogeymen he'd no desire to meet . . .

He'd managed to keep the lid down firmly on these jittery nerve-endings until the business was settled and, if anything, they'd lent a sharper edge to his negotiating skills so that he'd screwed a better bargain out of Cavendish than he had originally hoped for. Not perhaps as good as she would have got, given her head, but on the British end of the deal he'd preferred to keep her out of it. Over there, he'd told her when they were still in New York, they're not used to women making commercial decisions even when they're married to them. She'd only commented contemptuously that was because their wives were bird-brained dumbos who wouldn't know a balance sheet from a bank statement, and would be unable to read either. But at least she'd agreed to take a back seat on condition that she made the trip with him. As usual, she'd done the travel arrangements; only afterwards had he found out she'd bought one-way tickets...

Now he drew up a chair opposite to her, put down his briefcase and opened it, spreading the papers in front of her.

'Here's the contract, signed, sealed and delivered. Want to look at it?'

'Later,' she said, examining her fingertips which were an opalescent red and caught the sun's rays only to trap and kill them. 'I'll take your word for it. You're not a fool, Gerry. But contracts only need signing—sealing and delivering is for documents, as you should know by this time. How long?'

'Before the money's in the bank?' He knew quite well what she meant. 'By the end of the week. And there's an extra ten thousand in commission coming our way.' It was a small boast, though he knew she wouldn't be impressed.

'Peanuts,' she said, as expected. 'But I suppose you earned it.'

'We both did.' It was doubly necessary now to placate her, her mood was uncertain. 'Half the proceeds will be banked here in London, half in the States.'

Her eyes flared.

'You said it was to be all over here...'

'I changed my mind. Look, honey, it's best we keep on the New York apartment—for the time being.'

'I've already put it into the hands of Dominion Realty—with instructions to sell.'

'You didn't tell me. I certainly thought we'd be going back.'

'Well, now you know different. I've made all the arrangements with Leroy to close the office and transfer the assets.' She relaxed, spread her hands. 'Oh, what the hell—the Big Apple's gone mouldy. You said so yourself. It was our chance to sell out, and we took it.'

'But not to stay over here, damn you—and certainly not now.' He got up and went across to the drinks cabinet. The sun wasn't over the yardarm but he jolly well deserved it.

She was glancing at the contract, flicking the pages, but she would be taking in every word. She'd already been through the drafts as with a razor blade, spotting weaknesses, altering, discarding, until she'd finally approved the heads of agreement.

'It's OK.' She tidied the pages, put them back carefully in the case, yawned. 'Pour me one of these.'

As he handed her drink she looked up at him with her wise black eyes narrowed. 'What d'you mean—certainly not now?'

'For God's sake, Quin, answer that yourself. Look what's happened since we came to bloody England!'

'I'll thank you not to swear at the land of my birth—and you a patriotic soldier-man!'

'Honestly, Quin, we have to talk . . .'

'What about?'

'For one thing, this crazy idea of yours that we stay, that we don't go back to the States.'

'It's not crazy, and it's what I want. And, kid yourself not, Gerry Bulett, what I want I get. Or hadn't you noticed?' She swirled round in her seat, and began singing in an execrable high falsetto: 'London pride is my own dear town to me . . .'

'Shut up!' he roared. At any other time he'd have found it grotesque, this music-hall turn she put on; now that she had told him about Alma Street, he found it frightening.

'Don't shout at me, you two-bit con man,' she said through her teeth. 'Majors of your sort are two a penny in good old London Town, that's what you can't bear... If it hadn't been for me, you'd have ended up a down-at-heel salesman sporting phoney medals you never earned—that's if they'd ever let you out of clink...'

So it was out at last, the unspoken. In a way he was glad. She had so thoroughly expunged the past from both their lives that, once back in England, he had begun to feel he was living in an unreal world, and the speed with which she had acted to further extinguish all trace of that past had only thrown him deeper into a kind of helpless limbo.

Of course he'd watched her work fast before, and relished the audacity she'd brought to the wheeling and dealing which had taken their partnership into the highest echelons of American business—nor had he been averse to enjoying the riches it had brought.

And she was right; it was she who had made it possible.

People had often remarked to him what a complex, clever lady his wife was. She wasn't complex at all if you believed in the purity of the power motive. She was simple as an amoeba when it came to survival... She was the supreme egoist. To her mind, all mankind was base; words like principle, ethic, ideal were not within her range, she believed all action sprang from self-interest. Swift in decision, aided by a phenomenal memory for detail, a capacity for ingesting information like a well-fed computer, and an unerring skill in seeking out the weak spot in opponents, she'd carved her way through better brains than hers, inhibited as they were by sentimental attachments to conscience.

She was swearing at him now in the gutter language of her girlhood; she lapsed into it easily enough. He'd heard her use it as a safety-valve after a difficult business meeting, and he'd put up with it for the rewards her success at that meeting would bring. Sometimes he'd thought that he'd even acquired a taste for low life—as perhaps his antecedents had done when they'd trawled the streets of London for whores.

Not that Queenie was ever a whore in any sense of the word, there'd been no prostitution of talents for her...

He cut in on her harsh, screeching voice.

'It's all your fault for digging up the past. We both knew it was better left alone. That's why we've never spoken about it. What the hell did you have to go back there for?'

'And if I hadn't gone?' Fury dropped from her as quickly as it had come. 'What would have happened? It wasn't me who was digging up the past, it was that man I heard in the pub... What if he'd got to Larry before I did? Answer me that, Mr Know-all...'

He couldn't answer. He didn't know enough. She'd never told him everything... Twenty years ago when it had happened, she'd shut up like a clam, and it had suited him to leave it like that.

But this was different.

'There'll have to be an inquest. Have you thought about that?' he said, trying to bring his mind back to the present.

'Nothing to think about,' she said briskly, at her best when it came to practical matters. 'Poor Larry took his own dismal life, or he had an unfortunate accident when he was blind drunk... I shan't send a wreath this time, if that's what you're on about. I never liked the bastard, anyway. Larry the Lamb, those giggling girls called him. Did you know that?' She gave a giggle herself. 'His pathetic little snuggery there in the basement. Roll over on the rug, me darlin', while I make us a nice cuppa tea... Well, that was one night too many for Larry, handsome Larry, the boy for the girls...'

He didn't know whether she was referring to the night she'd—what? Behind a barrier in his mind suspicion was growing, though he would not let it through... Or that other night, all those years ago, about which his memory, from long disuse, was still not clear.

One thing was certain. She had finished with Larry, he would be put in his grave as Amanda Richards had been, and she would not give them another thought. One of the secrets of her success in business was this quick dismissal from the mind, the ability she had to give a matter intense concentration, plan, execute, then forget ... No recriminations, no looking back.

But he could see now from the dark, brooding look on her face that perhaps the matter of Larry Lanscombe was not so easily to be put aside, and he felt chilled.

He had difficulty in finding the words. 'What did Larry say to you—about that night?'

She turned her head and looked at him, her eyes opaque, but he knew her of old, there were thoughts racing behind them.

'It's well you should ask,' she said slowly. 'We both had been sure he was on his own ... He never let on, did he?'

'Let on about what?' That damned cold feeling in his stomach was growing.

'That he had a girl with him.'

Gerry Bulett shivered. He looked at her in horror.

She gazed back, then laughed. 'What are you worried about? Haven't I always had the luck of the devil?'

NINETEEN

DOROTHEA COPELAND DISLIKED the months of February and March, still cold enough to be winter but not cosy enough to be enjoyed *as* winter. Neither-one-thing-nor-the-other months her mother had called them, and Dorothea agreed with her.

This year the end of February had been particularly dislikeable. Earlier there had been a week of surprising sunshine, even warmth, so that people went about looking hopeful, and birds sang. Then a bitter east wind set in, rain fell incessantly from scowling grey clouds, and the days darkened down as if for another winter.

Dorothea had always been affected by weather, and showed it.

'Cheer up, Dot, it'll soon be spring,' Charles had said that morning, pulling his overcoat around his shoulders. 'You feeling all right?' he added anxiously.

'Of course I am, just chilly.' She smiled, and kissed him, pleased that he at least had been more cheerful of late. And it was true that there was nothing physically wrong with her—she hadn't had a migraine in weeks. She watched Charley trotting round to the garage for the car, and thought how thankful she should be; Ian had passed those exams and both father and son felt enhanced by their respective contributions to that success.

But once indoors, and alone, Dorothea could not shake off those emanations from the past which still troubled her nights with dreams, and her days with sudden images that came fluttering at the edges of her vision. It was as if, having been recalled from that hidden recess of her mind, they refused to go away.

It's because of Amanda's death, she told herself, that I keep thinking of Larry Lanscombe. They've both been connected to that one period of my life, and so they go on cropping up together. Perhaps it's my way of trying to keep Mandy alive... But, her rational self argued, I have lots of other memories of Mandy, more recent and much happier. It's what Mandy told me that last day we had lunch, that crazy story about Queenie... Dorothea paused on the landing, whisking the cord of the vacuum-cleaner out of the way and leaning on the handle. And that terrible card... Someone, somewhere, playing a joke? Mandy might have had friends with macabre tastes, could that be it?

Queenie stared out from the dark entrance to the bedroom door. Squat and yellow-faced, she peered at Dorothea from lively black eyes, alight with mischief. So she had looked in those days, a figure fit to send the typists into nervous giggling, but quick to deprive them of further joy by the biting remark, the jab of pseudo-Cockney wit that sent some into hysterical laughter, others into sullen silence. On their weaknesses she was spot on, she'd wormed out their secrets, she traded on their adolescent insecurity, set one against the other till the little office seethed with incipient rivalry. But she got the work out of them.

Only Dorothea had stood apart, torn and made wretched, unable to throw off the horrible atmosphere—she could still find no words to describe it—which pervaded the whole ramshackle outfit that was Higgs Electric from the basement below the street to the flimsy den where Major Bulett sat issuing impossible orders, and angrily fending off importunate wives. Nothing had prepared Dorothea Lingard for her encounters with such awful people, with their shabby lives and sordid secrets...

Now she set her teeth, switched on the motor and pushed the cleaner into every nook and cranny of the stairs. She had found that by doing her housework with the grim determination of a soldier on an assault course—as if the act of polishing furniture or cutting vegetables required every resource of mind and body—she could keep those unwelcome forms and outlines at bay. No abstraction, she told herself severely, no gazing into space, for that was where the screen of memory came alive . . .

Charles would not be home for lunch today, so she would take her basket on wheels—a rather unimaginative Christmas gift from Ian—and walk to the supermarket in Newtown's centre square. She got out her good gabardine raincoat and waterproof headscarf—which made her think fleetingly of Mandy's brave scarlet chiffon—and left the house.

It was colder than she had thought, although the rain had stopped, and there was a leaden sky that seemed to be simply taking a breather before unleashing the next downpour. The store was warm, and she lingered even when she had bought all she needed. Through the turnstiles and out into the forecourt she wheeled her basket, a method of conveyance she wasn't yet used to and found awkward, afraid for other people's ankles and her own legs, which were delicate.

She stood, irresolute, wondering if it would not be nicer to have a sandwich and coffee in town rather than push her shopping home, by which time she would possibly be too tired to eat.

As she hesitated, the wind blew across the square, piling up plastic bags in corners and chilling her cheekbones so that she pulled her headscarf closer round her face, and felt suddenly forlorn.

It was then that Lennox Kemp saw her, and thought she looked like some refugee, bewildered in a strange land.

He was striding out vigorously from his office in search of food, shelter and warmth which he knew could be found in his favourite restaurant down the next street. He felt he owed it to himself to have a good meal to bolster up his sense of worth, which had somehow been dented by the morning's experiences.

The inquest on Lawrence Lanscombe had been scheduled for eleven o'clock at Edmonton Magistrates' Court. Because he felt guilty about wasting Gillorns' time on a frolic of his own—the term was a legal one and meant no disparagement of the serious nature of inquests—he had got up early and put in two hours' work at the office before driving to Edmonton.

The proceedings in fact had been short and to the point. On being presented with the evidence, and having heard the few witnesses who spoke, the Coroner had summed up briskly but sympathetically, and found that death had occurred through misadventure. He pointed out the obvious dangers of mixing properly prescribed medicinal remedies with any consumption of alcohol, but did not pontificate too heavily on the subject. This was rather surprising since the Coroner was not only lawyer and doctor but also a total abstainer; perhaps he had in mind the feelings of the darts team, some of whom were shuffling their feet at the rear of his Court.

Apart from the ambiguous manner of his death, the character of Larry Lanscombe came cleanly out of it, attested for by his workmates and his employer, and there was no hint that his life had been other than exemplary, if dull.

Sergeant Lucas caught Kemp's eye as they left the Court, and winked.

'Nought there for an eager beaver like yourself, Mr Kemp.'

'A charitable verdict,' said Kemp primly. 'However, if anything should crop up, perhaps Inspector Inskip will get in touch with me.'

Lucas raised an eyebrow. 'We've enough crime in our manor without going out looking for it,' he said, but Kemp knew the hint had been taken.

The only two women in Court had been Mrs McIlvey, and a stout motherly person who had given evidence as Larry's neighbour, and who had wept copiously. 'It's mostly nerves,' said Grace McIlvey to Kemp, but not unkindly. 'Milly's just realized that poor Larry might've blown the whole house up with all the gas there was about—and hers would've gone up too... Ted would've come today but he's still got that chest,' she went on, voluble now the ordeal of the inquest was over. 'The manager at the timber-yard's been a proper gent—he's getting their solicitor to clear up what Larry left. There won't be much, a few savings, and the house of course. He's asked Milly and me if we'll go through the stuff in there since there's no one else... It'll all go to the jumble, I shouldn't wonder. When I think of the pride Mrs Lanscombe took in that parlour of hers... Doesn't do to set such store by things... I've told them where she's laid in the churchyard of the old parish, and that's where Larry'll go beside her. Well, I'd best be getting back to Ted.'

An unhappy business, thought Kemp as he drove away, even after that merciful verdict. He felt no lifting of the weight on his mind.

And now here was someone looking even worse than he felt.

'Mrs Copeland! Isn't it a rotten day?' As if to confirm that no matter how bad it had been it could still get worse, the rain began again.

She turned round and saw him, brought the focus of her eyes back from whatever nowhere they had been fixed on, and exclaimed: 'Oh, Mr Kemp... Yes, how I hate this weather!'

'Charley's in London today, isn't he? He went off with a load of completions to do. Are you in town for lunch?'

She hesitated. 'I had rather thought of a sandwich some-where...'

'We can do better than that. There's a little restaurant round the corner I occasionally go to. Would you like to come? At least it'll get us out of this rain...'

He gave her no time even to think yea or nay. Before she fully realized it, he had seized the handle of the basket and was off, pushing it over the cobbles like a lawnmower. She found herself trotting by his side, half-laughing, half-apprehensive. She liked Mr Kemp but she was by nature shy, never entirely at her ease in the company of men, and inclined to revert, particularly when surprised, to a gauche girlishness which she deplored but could not help.

But once seated in the restaurant, a quiet family concern not given to pretentious decor, cosily homelike with white tablecloths and a small readable menu, she found herself relaxing.

'French people,' Kemp told her, 'no frills but the best food in Newtown—not that that's saying much.' He grinned at her. 'And it's warm. You looked so chilled standing out there.'

'I was,' she confessed, 'I was dithering. All these people rushing about...'

She accepted a sherry, felt its warmth flowing through her. 'It was as if I was on an island...'

'From which I rescued you.'

She had never before been conscious of Mr Kemp's charm, though she had heard others speak of it. What she had not expected, and therefore fell right into without being aware of it, was his complete absorption in her, and in what she had to say. No one that she could remember—not even Charles—had listened to her so lightly and yet so intently. Had she realized it, of course, she would have known that this was in essence the secret of charm, it being not so much an intrinsic quality in a person as an outgoing one, since it depends for its effect on someone else's reception and openness to it. Charm does not exist in a vacuum. The particle physicists call 'charm' draws other particles to it, and may be nothing on its own.

As the lunch proceeded, and Dorothea savoured the pleasure of a meal she had not herself planned, bought and cooked—a rare occurrence for her—she found herself talking without her normal inhibition and, as sometimes happens in chance encounters where neither party has prepared themselves for a tête-à-tête, the conversation took unexpected twists and turns.

Although they started with general topics at surface level, they were soon discussing their respective attitudes to life, and to people. They talked about loneliness and the self-sufficiency it could bring, how one could still be lonely in a crowd if that crowd ran counter to one's own view, or mood. 'Keeping thought to itself,' was how Kemp put it, and was surprised by her quick understanding of the concept. She was quite deep, this wife of Charley's, and he gently probed at what had made her so, her early life and the things that had mattered to her then.

'I liked working for Mr Allardyce,' she said at one point, 'and he wanted me to stay on, but his secretary had only been off sick . . . It wouldn't have been fair.'

'So you didn't take advantage?'

'Oh no. That would have been wrong. Anyway, it was Mr Allardyce who told me about the position at Gillorns, and gave me such a good reference that I easily got the job.'

'And met Charles?' Kemp was smiling at her with warm grey eyes.

'Yes,' she said, smiling in return, and he thought how beautiful she must have been at—what?—twenty or so?

'So, you've always worked for solicitors?'

'A few temporary places before. Nothing that mattered.'

It was a hurried remark, slurred over as she took a sip of wine. She was not used to it, but then neither was she used to talking about herself.

'But you liked legal work?'

'It suited me, I suppose. I love accuracy, you see . . . and tidiness, and order in things. Also, I seem to have this memory . . .'

'What sort of memory? I'm interested to know,' he added, seeing her hesitate.

'Well, I think they have a term for it . . . Instant recall. I keep remembering things . . . even little things, years afterwards.'

'Good lord, I wish I'd had you as a secretary! So many of them can't remember the letters I sent out yesterday!' As he uttered this calumny, Kemp gave a silent apology to his faithful Elvira.

'You must have been at Gillorns the same time as our Mr Stoddart,' he said casually. 'He would have been an articled clerk in your time.'

'I never worked for Mr Stoddart,' said Dorothea quickly, 'and I never thought he was a good influence on Charley. They came from different backgrounds even though they'd been friends.'

'They didn't remain friends, did they?'

'It wasn't to be expected. Their lives would go on different paths, Mr Kemp.' When Dorothea guarded her tongue, her speech took on a stilted primness.

'My dear Dorothea, why so formal? Surely you can call me Lennox by now. I'm sure Charley wouldn't mind.'

She laughed, nervously but with enjoyment. 'I don't think you're trying to seduce me. It's just that I'm not used to all this attention . . .'

It was clear to Kemp that under this attention Dorothea was blossoming—there was no other word for it. Her great dark blue eyes had softened into a lambent tenderness at variance with the tight lines round her nose and mouth which betrayed habitual restraint.

He asked her if she liked living in Newtown, and, after a moment's reflection, she nodded.

'Charley's happier here than he was in London,' she answered. 'He likes working for you, Lennox—' She brought out the name as if testing it. 'You give him scope. He needs that. He can very easily be put down...'

Kemp wondered how much she knew about the quarrel with Stoddart, if she knew anything at all. He began to have a small conscience about discussing her husband, so he took refuge in generalities.

'Work matters,' he said. 'You must have been aware of that in your early office days. People tend to forget that eight hours or so of every day are spent in a certain atmosphere, with certain people you can't just shake off, you're forced to be with them, sometimes in a confined space. It can be worse than a bad marriage.'

'That's clever of you to recognize it. Not a lot of employers do. I can help Charley because I know what he goes through when things go wrong. When people are... well, antagonistic...'

'Like Mr Stoddart?'

The waiter had approached, offering sweets. They chose, and Dorothea took a little time, but resumed the conversation where it had been left off.

'I'm glad you know about Mr Stoddart,' she said. 'And Charley's so much better now.'

'Did he tell you about it?'

She shook her head. 'I only guessed that it was Mr Stoddart being in the same office that was getting Charley down.'

'A matter of long-standing hostility?'

She tightened her lips, and would not be drawn.

'I don't know anything about that. Only that you took Charley's part, and I'm grateful...'

Again Kemp tried the philosophic approach. 'As I was saying, for many people work is the most important thing in their lives. They have to live within its range, for good or bad. It has its influence on the whole way they conduct their lives, that terrible day-to-day existence.'

'Why do you say, terrible . . . Lennox?'

'Because it can be.'

She was breaking up her choice of meringue chantilly with the little fork and spoon.

'A long time ago,' she said, raising her eyes but not looking at him, and seeing something far beyond the walls of the restaurant, 'I knew the truth of what you've just said, that terrible day-to-day thing . . .'

'Tell me about it, Dorothea.'

'There was this dreadful shabby office, and people you couldn't live with . . . And the presence of something that I can only call . . . evil. You had to go in, day after day, knowing they would be there . . .' Her eyes were dark as she saw it all again. 'You began to have feelings you didn't know existed.' She stopped, then went on in a low murmur, 'And you still feel them when the . . . the scene . . . comes back.'

He tried to catch the words.

'Feelings of what?'

'Inadequacy, fear . . . Oh, I don't know. I can't express it. Hatred. I suppose.'

'That's a strong word, hatred.'

'But that's what it was. That's what it amounted to.'

'Hatred of what? Of a person?'

'All of them, but especially one . . . Queenie.' She breathed the name.

'Who was this Queenie?'

'The personification of evil.' Dorothea had finished the wine. Already her mind was spinning, but the words came tumbling out as clear as the images she was seeing. 'A rat from the gutter, just as Mandy always said. But Mandy didn't care, she was strong. But I cared . . . I couldn't help myself. Have you ever hated anyone, Lennox, really hated?'

Whatever Kemp had expected of Dorothea Copeland it was not this. Not those burning eyes, brimming with long-felt resentment, dangerous eyes betraying thoughts deeply hidden till now. But her words were not making any sense to him.

'Mandy, that was your friend, Amanda, the one who died?'

'Yes, yes, Mandy...' Dorothea was excited now. 'She had this crazy story...that Queenie was still alive...that she didn't die in that awful...' But even now Dorothea could not bring herself to say the word, for if she did then the worst image of all would rise up before her eyes and she wouldn't be able to bear it.

At that moment she wanted to tell Kemp everything, spill out her doubts and her fears, reach back into the storehouse of her memory and pull things off the shelves for his inspection. He would come up with a rational answer, he was sensible, a man with a clear brain, he would dismiss her lurking terrors, give her absolution...

But she stopped herself in time. She had been taught that you dealt with your own troubles, you cleaned up your own house, you did not invoke the aid of strangers. Besides, there was Charley. What would Charley think of her, taking her neurotic fancies to such as Mr Kemp? And what of the consequences? It would mean giving up her secret, the secret she'd kept even from Charley... How would that seem to him now, after all these years?

The restaurant swirled round Dorothea. The images were there, dancing like life-sized motes in her eyes: Mandy in the arms of Larry Lanscombe, Queenie stalking between the typewriters, Major Bulett's hard red face, and—what would surely break her—the thin wires stretched across the basement to that shoddy corner, and the spark that ran...

She bit down hard on her coffee spoon.

'I'm sorry,' she said, smiling the images away, 'you've given me too much to drink. I'm not used to it.' She gathered up her handbag, fussily, and took herself off, unsteadily, to the ladies' room. She splashed cold water repeatedly on her face, tidied her hair, stood a long time before the mirror composing her features and her mind with the same determination she brought to housework.

While he waited for her return Kemp wondered what she had been about to say, and why she had stopped. She had been on the verge of some disclosure, he was sure of that. He had seen too many people with problems on their minds, with troubled consciences and old secrets that had festered, wounds which would not heal, not to recognize the symptoms.

When she returned, he was paying the bill and, seeing her face, pale and with a set look to it as if she was ashamed of herself for spoiling his lunch, he found he could ask her nothing. For that was exactly what she said.

'I'm sorry I spoiled your lunch, Mr Kemp, running on the way I did. I can't think what came over me. Now I'd best get this lot of groceries home or the whole afternoon will be gone.'

'You're not pushing that contraption through this rain, Dorothea,' he told her firmly. 'My car's in the office car park. I'll run you back.' He ignored her protestations and would have gone for the car himself, leaving her in the shelter of the restaurant, but she insisted on accompanying him.

'You've already put yourself out for me,' she said, 'and it's good of you to run me home.'

They crossed the square and walked down the street to the car park at the rear of Gillorns. Kemp stowed the basket in the boot and opened the passenger door for Dorothea. As he did so, he glanced up at the windows of the office, more out of habit than anything else. Two figures moved behind the glass in Charles Copeland's room; young owl-eyed Mr Lambert dealing with one of Charley's clients in his absence. For Charley's sake Kemp hoped it meant a nicely lucrative conveyancing fee; that department's costs were rising splendidly, so that even Head Office had begun to mutter approval.

He said as much to Dorothea, who responded as any ordinary wife would on hearing a good report of her husband—and there was no doubt that is what she was again, an ordinary housewife with her own thoughts tightly bound up in her headscarf.

Kemp disliked this return to trivialities. His mind felt loose, disconnected. He found he couldn't talk to her at that level. He wondered briefly if it would divert her if he told her about the inquest he'd attended that morning. If he mentioned casually the name of the deceased would there be any reaction?

But she gave him no opportunity. The journey was a short one, and during it she prattled on about prices in the supermarket, vandalism in the town centre, and other banal topics which required the minimum response from him. She was warding him off, Kemp could sense it, building a defence of small talk, as if to say plainly the lunch-time interlude was over, they had returned to their own levels, and that was how she wanted them to remain.

When she had closed the gate she gave a little wave of the hand and the flicker of a smile before she started up the path, dragging her basket. In her mouse-coloured serviceable coat, the ends of her scarf flapping as she bent into the wind, she could have been any drab peasant woman back from a day's toil in the fields.

She has pretty ankles, though, Kemp said to himself as he drove away, and there's a lot more to Dorothea Copeland than meets the eye.

He could not have said how it was that she should invoke such a feeling of disquiet. He looked back once at the neat house, secure behind its trim hedges, out of the wind's and the rain's way.

TWENTY

WHEN TONY LAMBERT hurried into Charles Copeland's room the client who had been sent there by the receptionist turned from the window.

'Not much of a view, is it?' she remarked, with a smile.

He crossed the room and stood beside her. 'It is a bit glum,' he agreed. 'A winter's day in Newtown isn't something you put on travel posters. I'm sorry I kept you waiting.'

'That's OK. I've been having a look round. This your office?'

'No. My name is Lambert. It will be our Mr Copeland who will handle your business, but he's in London this afternoon, so...'

'Why, surely that's Mr Kemp,' she interrupted him. She was still gazing out of the window.

Tony peered down at the car park.

'Yes, it's Mr Kemp. Do you know him?'

'We haven't actually met,' she replied, vaguely, 'and I suppose that's his wife with him. Looks like he's been helping her with the shopping.'

'Mr Kemp isn't married.' Tony looked again. 'No, that's Mrs Copeland.'

'Another man's wife?' she said, brightly, then laughed. 'I didn't mean it quite that way...' She walked slowly towards the desk where Tony was hastily clearing space for himself and searching in the drawers for a notebook. 'If this is Mr Copeland's room, that'll be him and his family?'

Tony glanced owlishly at the small framed photograph of a young couple with a child on the sands at some seaside

resort. It stood on the shelf above the radiator flanked by
two large volumes on Town and Country Planning. 'Yes, it
is, but it must have been taken years ago...'

'I'll say! Just look at their clothes... Those terrible mini-
skirts!' She sat down, and smoothed the folds of black velvet which fell to below her calves. The gesture drew young
Lambert's attention to her costume. That's a stylish suit, he
thought, bang up to date, and must have cost a packet. Although he was immured for much of his time within the
desiccated limits of his beloved trusts, Tony was no slouch
when it came to assessment of women, or their clothes.

'I'm awfully sorry you had to wait,' he apologized again,
'We're in a bit of a rush this afternoon with Mr Copeland
and Mr Kemp both out, and I'm afraid I was on the telephone when you arrived for your appointment.' He pushed
his spectacles more firmly on to the bridge of his nose, and
prepared to be businesslike. 'Now, as I understand it, you're
intending to buy the property called Broxburn Hall. As a
matter of fact I know it. It's a beautiful place.' Damn it,
he'd forgotten to get the woman's name from Anna in reception. 'Phoned this morning... Urgent conveyancing...
Big property in Hertfordshire. You'll have to see her, Mr
Lambert, there's nobody else free,' Anna had hissed at him
when he got back from lunch.

'A beautiful place,' he said, again.

'Yes, young man, it is. And a beautiful price, too... But
what the hell does that matter? My husband and I, we're
retiring from business, retiring to the country...'

She gave him her name, and the interview proceeded like
any other.

Charley'll be pleased with this one, thought young Mr
Lambert when the client had departed, leaving behind in the
rather gloomy dark room a faint whiff of perfume, wholly
Parisian, wholly out of place in Newtown on a winter afternoon.

But the next morning it had vanished, lost in the healthy antiseptic smells brought in by the cleaning ladies.

And certainly never noticed by Charles Copeland, for he had gone straight home from the London train which didn't get in till after six o'clock. He was tired, but full of the quiet satisfaction which follows a good day's work. The completions of transactions by City companies prudently investing funds in Newtown's growing industrial areas, as well as a run of sales and purchases for individuals, would bring Charles's monthly costs up to a new high.

These latter clients might never set eyes on their titles to property, for the documents would join the merry-go-round from one building society to another—tripping in and out of the Land Registry on the way—without ever pausing at the houses in between.

Charles regretted the passing of old title deeds, now economically pressed into the single Land or Charge certificate which lacked, for him, the glamour of ancient vellum, and the archaic abbreviations of the abstracts of title upon which he had cut his teeth as a young conveyancing clerk. They still came in occasionally from the more backward provinces, but where Charles now worked time was of the essence; the completion process which scrutinized the vendor's right to sell and the purchaser's adequacy to buy the hereditaments bargained for, had accelerated to the point where many considered it mere formality so long as the money was right. Not Charley. He still went his slow, careful way, leaving nothing to chance, be it a trustee's signature missing on a deed, or a light fixture missing on a staircase. A stickler for detail, some called him with respect; others a nitpicking old humbug, without it.

Today there had been no snags, and as he put his key in the door and smelled the aroma of a welcoming supper he might have echoed the John Denver song that it was good to be back home again... But if he saw any warm light in his wife's eyes he did not comment on it. In fact he took very little notice of Dorothea as she went about preparing the meal. Dorothea was there, as she always was, in the house that was swept and tidy, setting our plates and dishes, the handmaiden of his modest needs.

'Let's have some wine with dinner,' he said, surprising himself with the suggestion. 'There's that bottle the Evanses brought back from Spain for us . . . I feel I've earned it today,' he added, to explain the unusual conviviality.

'Well.' She stopped what she was doing, and stared. 'This is a day for drinking. But why not?'

With the food on the table, he poured her a glass and took his own. But it was half way through the meal before he said: 'What did you mean, Dot, about a day for drinking?' He might be slow in taking it in but he always listened to a remark of Dorothea's, no matter how inconsequential.

'Oh, just that I've had wine already today.'

She told him about her meeting with Mr Kemp.

'What on earth did you find to talk about, my pet?'

'I can't honestly remember . . .' Which was true, for the conversation was blurred in her mind now, though she knew important things had been said, and some left unsaid.

'It was decent of him to take you out,' Charles remarked when she had told him what she remembered, but not all of it. 'I must thank him.'

'There's no need. He did it out of casual kindness, I think. He has that easy way with him.'

She cleared the table, brought coffee to the sitting-room, and they sat companionably side by side to finish the wine.

'He mentioned Stoddart,' she said, 'and asked if I'd known him back at Gillorns when I worked there.'

Charles frowned. 'I never told Mr Kemp you had been in Gillorns' office.'

'Well, I suppose Nick did.'

'Surely all that business is over,' Charles said shortly.

'Will it ever be over, Charley? Really over—so that we can forget it?'

'Damn Stoddart, bringing it up like he did! It's finished. And you'd nothing to do with it, Dottie . . . remember that.'

'I helped, didn't I?'

'Only because I asked you to. And don't think I haven't regretted that as much as the other thing... But it's over. I've had it out with Mr Kemp, and in many ways I'm glad. My conscience is clearer than it was.'

'The virtue of absolution.' Something bleak in her voice made Charles look at her sharply.

'Dorothea,' he said, and it wasn't often he used her full name, 'don't for heaven's sake go brooding on something that's past and gone. It was my mistake, taking that money, I fully acknowledge it. I should never have done it, and I've always been sorry that I involved you.'

She meditated on that for a moment. She knew that he meant it, though he'd not actually admitted it before. They had, as it were by mutual but unspoken agreement, decided they would never refer again to what had happened. He had his reasons, so had she.

'I think,' she said now, slowly picking at her thoughts to put them into words, 'I think Mr Kemp knows all about it . . .'

'Of course Kemp knows, I had to tell him... And he'd get the rest from Stoddart.'

'I don't mean only that. I think he knows that I was . . . involved in some way . . .'

'How could he know?' exclaimed Charles fiercely. 'Oh, I suppose that was Stoddart again. He had a grudge against you, too. The bastard! After all this time... Why'd he have to bring you into it? All you'd done was the typing... Surely Kemp didn't accuse you?'

'Of course not. Mr Kemp isn't like that. I think he'd work it out for himself, that one of the typists missed out parts of the evidence . . .' She stopped. She could see as if the pages were held up before her the paragraphs in the assessors' first report, the brief but damning words in the interview with the storeman, the name leaping at her: Lawrence Lanscombe. Then, obliteration... Into the shredding machine, sheared down to meaningless strips. She felt Charley's eyes upon her, and recovered. 'Anyway, Nick would tell him. We both knew how Nick felt... And meeting you again, perhaps he wanted revenge... on both of us.'

'Well, it got him nowhere.' Charles calmed down. 'I'm only sorry Mr Kemp had to know about your part in it. But he'll understand. He told me himself that he knew what it was like to be without money in an emergency. He gave in to the pressure just as I did. He pinched trust moneys to cover his wife's debts... And it was such a little thing you did, and you did it for me, love.'

It was not often these days that Charley indulged in what he would have called sentiment, but partly out of his previous contentment, partly out of relief that things were being said openly that had long remained battened down, he did so now. 'You did it for me, Dottie, and I loved you for it then as I love you to this day...' He put his arm round her shoulders, and gave her a hug.

Dorothea was comforted by the embrace, knowing it went to the heart of their marriage, that dependence on each other which knitted them together into a single fabric stretched, if necessary, against all comers. If one strand should give, she thought, the whole might unravel. Yet she had to voice misgiving, as if to surrender all of herself might bring down fate upon them both. If she spoke out now, could such fate be averted?

'Mr Kemp,' she began hesitantly, 'when he talks... he gives you the impression he can see right through you... It's unnerving. He throws you off-balance, somehow... It's as if he know more about what's going through your mind than you know yourself...'

Charles tightened his hold on her.

'It's only a technique he uses on his more devious matrimonial clients, Dottie darling. It doesn't concern us. And, come to think of it, he lives a lonely enough life, perhaps he envies us because he isn't as happy as we are.'

LENNOX KEMP certainly wasn't happy that night going home to his nondescript flat where, as he sometimes put it, he lived inside his head so that his surroundings were of little consequence. He had taken with him from the office the dusty bundle of papers in the case of Edmonton Mutual Assurance and, after a scratch supper, he settled down with it as with an old, rather boring acquaintance who might yet come up with a nugget of inspirational gossip.

He peeled the pages back, one by one, and searched the words, and the gaps in the words. It was like the dotted pictures he'd filled in as a child, joining numbers, making a giraffe or a little house with trees.

He got himself a drink, and considered houses—which effectively removed him from the typescript and took him into the territory of his not inconsiderable imagination.

No. 43 Balaclava Terrace with its sad laburnum, and sadder, lonely death, had been bought with tainted money. 'Say nothing, Larry lad, and I'll see you're all right.' That sounded like the gallant Major, but a rare type indeed to cover up misfeasance on somebody else's part. He'd wanted no trouble, settle the matter quickly, and don't let the sparks fly upwards... His superiors had seen it differently, they had a good name to preserve, and they were breathing down his neck. Kemp felt a certain sympathy for the ex-manager of Higgs Electric; his own head office had the same effect on him from time to time. Loftily removed from the scene of action, they too would go in, all big guns firing and devil take the hindmost.

So the Major had done a bit of sabotage. Why? Not surely just to protect Larry Lanscombe, a menial store-keeper in his early twenties. And pay him a thousand pounds? For what? Why go to such lengths for this young dab hand at electrical installation if by his negligence he'd caused a fire in which someone had died?

Kemp's mind wandered to that other house, Charles and Dorothea Copeland's first, bought with the aid of a bribe so that they could marry and have their baby. The offer had come at a desperate time for them, and the temptation had been too much. Charles he could understand . . . but Dorothea? Something there was wrong. Kemp felt it as Nick Stoddart had done. Dorothea Lingard, a highly-principled young lady, had stooped, had connived at misconduct, and she hadn't been an ignorant girl, she'd known exactly what she was doing.

Too delicate a question to ask, was she really pregnant as Nick had implied, or had that simply been further mischief-making on his part? Perhaps it had always been something unspoken of, and still was. Trouble that lay too deep for words might easily close down the lid on iniquity. Perhaps the Major had just been lucky in his timing. Perhaps the Devil was looking after his own.

Kemp was a great priser open of lids if he thought justice could be served by doing so, but too often justice was a two-edged sword, cutting the innocent even as it slew the guilty.

Why not give up the whole thing? As everyone kept telling him, it all happened a long time ago, and the sordid little misdeeds that had been done were buried in these dusty papers in front of him, just as surely as the evidence of the fire was buried under the brash new buildings in Alma Street.

He got himself another drink, prowled round the flat, threw himself down once more and pulled the file towards him. It told him nothing new; any careful lawyer could have spotted the gaps but Fenimore had been elderly, he had competent assistants and more important matters on his own desk. Stoddart had stood aside. He'd taken no money, his fingers were clean, he'd cynically relished the intrigue, probably been jolly glad to get a lever on Charles who'd stolen his girl . . .

His girl. A complex creature, as Kemp had discovered today, a woman capable of more intense feelings than one would guess from her prim demeanour. She had talked of hatred . . . of evil . . .

Kemp was suddenly swept again into that state of frustrated despondency he'd experienced when he'd come out of the Inkerman Arms and walked down Balaclava Street. Only now it was worse, for with it had come a sense of dangerous urgency as if he were being stalked by a beast that lurked but had not yet chosen the moment to spring.

He must turn and face the doubt that had to be rooted out ere he could let the matter rest, drag from the back of his mind where it had been lying in wait the terrible question of his own responsibility.

Had it been the sight of his card with that telltale name of Gillorns, both a reminder and a threat, which had pushed poor Larry Lanscombe to the point of suicide?

It was a bitter thought; it made Kemp feel like a murderer.

TWENTY-ONE

DOROTHEA WAKENED the next morning into a curious state of mind, carried over as it were from her dreams which continued to surface with startling clarity even in the light of day.

This had happened to her before, so that when the little episodes came and went, although she knew them to be fragments of dreams, they were as real to her as the cups and saucers she was setting down on the draining-board. She usually countered these sensations with a no-nonsense attitude which shooed them away, back into nothingness.

But today was different. She felt light-headed, and her body flimsy, full of a strange anticipation bordering on panic. She leant on the sink and stared out into the garden, at the winter grass and the privet hedge, the top leaves just caught and twitching in the wind. Her dreams had been no more strange than at other times, bits of this and that, figures she didn't know, and some she recognized, all talking to her though she couldn't hear them, for sound never entered that other world. Yet she knew the tenor of their silent mouthings. Warning. Concerned anxiety. They were worried about her, they were trying to tell her something. It had happened before. She'd dreamed of Larry that way, but Larry hadn't appeared to her last night.

Amanda was there. In the green dress she'd worn the night she'd taken Dorothea to that fortune-teller down in Hackney. 'She's ever so good, Freckles,' Amanda had said. 'She'll do the cards or you can have the crystal...' Dorothea had smiled at her friend. 'You know I don't go in for that kind of rubbish...' But she'd been persuaded to go.

That old woman's face, all greasy and with swart hairs on the upper lip had been in the dream last night. Not of course as she had been in reality, sitting in that dingy parlour with the tatty velvet cloth on the table. 'Your pal's a sceptic,' she'd said to Mandy, 'doesn't believe a word...' Which had been true. Only as the two girls went out she'd come to the door and grabbed Dorothea's arm, pulled her back and said. 'You want to watch it, you ... Didn't anybody ever tell you you're a bit psychic yourself? If you hear the warning, don't run away from it...'

In the alley outside Mandy and Dorothea had collapsed in fits of giggles. 'The gipsy's warning!' Mandy was choking with laughter. 'I get the tall dark stranger, and all you get's the gipsy's warning!'

Remembering the incident now, Dorothea felt more than ever like a character in a novel—a phrase she'd picked up but which meant nothing since neither she nor Charley read novels. He preferred non-fiction, books about eminent people—and not too many of those. Had she known it, it was a thing which had struck Lennox Kemp when he'd visited their house—the lack of books. It needn't denote lack of imagination, he'd said to himself, and people can lead happy enough lives without knowing how to pronounce Proust, never mind read him...

When Dorothea thought about being a character in a novel she only meant that she was outside herself, watching. It was a sensation not unknown to her, she seemed to be lighter than her body and free of it while it went about its customary tasks, cleaning the heavy clay from the potatoes, peeling them round and round, popping them into water, slitting leeks and slicing onions with sharp knives from the collection Charley'd set up in the pinewood holder on the kitchen wall.

The milkman came, the postman, and the man to read the gas. She took the rubbish out to the bin. It was cold in the garden and she was glad she didn't have to do any shopping. There was a staff meeting at the office today, so Charley wouldn't be in for lunch. She'd have a sandwich for herself, and then get out the paper pattern for that skirt she was going to cut out. She'd make a casserole for supper with those vegetables she'd got ready and the steak in the fridge. What about afters? She reached up for a tin of peaches, or rather her arm did as her other self watched. *That'll be the last time she'll be in the larder*... Dorothea brought the tin down slowly, thoughtfully, and crossed to use the opener on the opposite wall. *She won't use that again*... Dorothea stood stock-still in the middle of the kitchen. Voices... Images flickered at the corners of her eyes. Damn it, she thought, not another migraine... Not now.

For that was how they often started, in heightened consciousness. Then the shadow. She could almost touch the shadow, like the fold of a curtain being gently but remorsely pulled across the line of her vision. And, as today, preceded by this feeling of lightness, the images in her head more real than her surroundings...

Mandy in the green frock with the absurd leather fringe trapped her as she looked in her needlework box for the skirt pattern and the pinking shears. Dorothea sat back on her heels and said aloud: 'Oh, please go away, Mandy, can't you see I'm busy?'

The telephone rang.

Dorothea glanced at the clock in the hall as she lifted the receiver. Half past eleven. Perhaps the meeting was off and Charley would be in to lunch. It would have to be omelettes, there were plenty of eggs, and there was always cheese.

'Is that Mrs Copeland?' A woman's voice, not one she knew. Probably another offer of double-glazing; there'd been a lot of them recently.

'Yes, this is Mrs Copeland.'

'I'm real sorry to bother you, Mrs Copeland. I was a friend of Amanda Egerton's back in the States. I've only just arrived in your country, and I've heard that she died...'

Dorothea shifted her position at the phone. She sat down on the padded bench that housed the directories and Charley's business diary. 'Yes?' she said.

'It was a real shock to me, Mrs Copeland. I got to know Amanda when she was in New York last year, and she made me promise I'd look her up if I ever came to London. I spoke with a man in that firm she worked for soon as I got here. My Gawd, was that a smack in the face! I can't tell you... I sure was grieved to find she'd died...'

'It was a shock to all of us,' said Dorothea, overwhelmed by the rush of words, the accent, the surprise.

'I'd just love to have a talk with you, Mrs Copeland. I've got to be back in the States in a coupla days, but I can't rest till I find out about Amanda. Talk to someone, you know? We became good friends over there, had a great time together. I can't believe she's gone, and I'd be real grateful if I could see you. I reckon you'd be her greatest friend. Now, I'd not want to go butting in if it isn't convenient. My name's Bettine Frazer. I'm only over here for a few days. I'm a buyer for Wanamaker's and they sure make me stick to a hard schedule...'

'I don't think... I can't possibly get into London...'

'Oh, I didn't mean for you to do that, honey. Look, I got a hire car, and those folks at the design place, they tell me Newtown's not that far out... I'd make it in no time.'

'I really don't know...' Dorothea hated this kind of unexpected interruption to routine, and did she really want to talk about Amanda? To a stranger?

'I guess it's an imposition,' the voice had softened. 'You're probably still upset about her passing away like she did... But I just can't get over it, you know? I only want to talk about her for mebbe an hour or two. She was a won-

derful person. She mentioned you several times...said what
a kind, understanding friend you'd been to her...'

It was a wheedling sort of flattery. Everyone likes to hear
good of themselves, and Dorothea was no exception. She
felt herself warming to this unknown caller.

'Wouldn't it be a trouble to you coming all the way out
here? There's the traffic, and you won't know the roads...'
She was flustered now, wanting to please.

'No trouble. I got maps. It's real nice of you, Mrs Copeland.' The tone had become brisk. 'Let's see. It's half eleven
now. I could be there by one. I've got your address in the
book. Don't bother fixing anything to eat. I'm on a diet,
anyway. Gee, I'm so grateful... I couldn't go back to the
States without a word...'

Although Dorothea knew few Americans, she had found
them, if anything, friendly to the point of being effusively
so to one of her temperament. She sensed they found her
uptight, unwilling, or perhaps unable, to relax in their
company. She would try and make amends for that... This
request was something she could not, out of courtesy, easily put aside.

'I will be at home all day,' she said, stammering a little,
'if you find it not too much trouble to come.' She gave
directions, explained where the house was in their road, and
put down the phone.

She must change her plans, make preparations for the
visit. At least that would keep her occupied, give her something to do, banish that scary feeling.

BY ONE O'CLOCK Dorothea had a tray ready with two cups
and saucers of her best china, the old-fashioned silver teapot, cream jug and sugar basin which had belonged to her
mother, and a small dish of sweet and plain biscuits. She put
it on the kitchen table. When she comes, she thought, I'll

carry it into the lounge, then I can be busy pouring out while she talks about Mandy. American women are very outgoing, they're more interested than we are in people they meet casually, and Mandy would have made an impact on anyone she met... She won't stay long. She's a business woman, she has a timetable to keep to. Why do I have to feel it's an ordeal? Why am I getting so jumpy? But I'm always this nervous when entertaining people. Charley says so.

She looked round the kitchen. She'd already done the lounge, arranged the chairs and the sofa, straightened the pictures, put fresh water in the few daffodils she'd bought last week, cut the stems and brought in a bit of evergreen from the garden. The kitchen too was neat and tidy, the surfaces shone, everything was in its proper place. Oh, that mallet shouldn't be in the corner by the waste-bin; Charley'd brought it in last night, he was going to fix the shaft. Said it had loosened when he was hammering in those stakes for the runner beans. She'd move it out to the shed, it wasn't right in the kitchen... And, heavens, that soapy water still in the sink! She'd used it to wash the china when she brought it from the glass cabinet in the lounge. I'd better run that away, she thought, starting towards it...

Too late.

She heard the purr of a car, saw from the window its black top sliding past above the hedge. She gave a hurried glance at herself in the mirrored tile she'd got Charley to put on the wall by the door; just to make sure my hat's straight when I go to the shops, she'd explained apologetically.

You're much too self-conscious, Dorothea, one of her schoolteachers had told her, don't you realize that's a form of vanity? Dorothea never considered herself vain.

Now she patted her hair with nervous fingers, and went into the hall just as the doorbell pealed.

The woman out on the step was smartly dressed. Dorothea took that in straight away, appraising the dark velvet suit under the short swinging fur, the perky little red hat with a brim half-covering the face.

'Please come in ... It's Mrs Frazer, isn't it?' Dorothea couldn't remember whether she'd said if she was Mrs or Miss.

'Bettine will do, honey ... for now.'

She was over the threshold almost before Dorothea could stand aside. Without turning, the incomer kicked the door shut behind her with the back of her foot, at the same time bringing a gloved hand out and up from the pocket of her coat. She held the hard black object in that hand firmly pointed at Dorothea's head.

'You and I are going to have a nice talk about Amanda—and other things,' she said with a grin.

Dorothea had never seen a real gun before—only in films or on the television. Disbelief gave way to simple astonishment, and to a reaction quicker than thought. She made for the closed front door. Queenie dealt her a sharp blow on the side of her ear with the small automatic, not too hard but enough to send her reeling, clutching for support at the wall.

'That's just for starters, kiddo. So you don't try any more funny business. Now, where can we talk in this little bunny-hutch of yours, eh?'

TWENTY-TWO

'WASN'T THAT A STROKE of luck, then, me going to the solicitors to find out what that Lennox Kemp kept nosing around for? Imagine you being married to Charley Copeland! Can't have that, you know. Too damned dangerous. Not you and Charley Copeland, both... That could mean trouble. Somebody clever putting two and two together, like that nosey-parker Kemp...'

Anyone looking in at the window would have seen two women having tea on a gloomy afternoon in a suburban kitchen where all was as it should be, sitting on steel chairs with blue vinyl seats, at a white plastic-topped table.

Dorothea's tea was cold in the cup but Queenie was enjoying hers, raising it to her thin, smiling lips with her left hand. The right hand in the black silk glove rested on the shining surface but the curled fingers were firm on the gun. Dorothea thought it looked out of place beside her mother's delicately embroidered teacosy. She had long given up any attempt at coherent reasoning. Her head ached where she'd been struck, and she felt blood trickling on to her neck, but the pain was nothing like migraine. I'm used to it, she said to herself fiercely, I know all about pain. I can stand it. She stared at Queenie from a blank, sullen face.

Queenie put down her cup. 'Ta, ever so,' she said. 'You still make a good cuppa. That was one of your jobs, wasn't it, duckie, back there at Higgs? Tea-girl and general dogsbody. The wonder was Larry the Lamb ever gave you the time of day.'

'Larry?' Dorothea got it out through stiff lips. 'What happened to Larry?'

'Oh, he killed himself. Gas oven. Very depressed he was, old Larry, after we'd had a chat. Only needed a shove in the right direction. He scared easy, did Larry... like all those years ago...' Queenie gave a hoot of a laugh. 'I'd heard him, see, in the basement, and I told the boss. Gerry soon got it out of him he'd been there, he'd get the blame...'

Dorothea shivered. It was all going to come out now, what she'd dreaded. Something strange was welling up inside her, not the usual tight knotted feeling, something almost like relief.

Queenie had slung off her coat, put the red hat cheekily on top of the salt crock. Her black hair was smooth and unruffled.

'Larry never said he'd a girl with him—not till t'other night when I guess I pressured him a little. You could have knocked me down with a feather when he told me it was Dorothea Lingard. What a sneaky, snivelling slyboots you were! I'd have reckoned on it being Amanda Richards. Funny, I never believed all that crap he gave the Major about working late on a repair job. Of course he'd denied hearing anyone else in the building, but Gerry and me, we couldn't take a chance on that, so Gerry paid him off. Wasn't hard. Larry was shit-scared about that wiring of his, fixing up his little lovers' nest in the storeroom...'

'Why did you have to come back?' muttered Dorothea. I've got to keep her talking, she thought feverishly, she's safe when she's talking. And Queenie always liked to talk, and she hasn't changed. That grating voice, the awful East End whine... She's got into Americanized slang but it's still the same hateful common voice.

'I like good old London town, ducks. And there's a nice big estate up in Hertfordshire we're going to buy. Fancy me as lady of the manor? Me from the back streets, eh? And I'm going to stay.' The hard eyes glittered. 'There's nobody now to stop me, hear that? You're the last, and I only came

on you by luck. Queenie's luck. Isn't that the cutest thing?
Amanda, Larry... and you.'

Dorothea swallowed. She kept telling herself to keep
calm. 'Mandy didn't know...' she said.

Queenie helped herself to a biscuit, crunching it between
her sharp white teeth. She shook her head.

'Couldn't afford the risk once she'd seen me and the Major. Thought she was being smart looking at the hotel register, but two can play at that game. She was out of luck,
your Mandy, from the time I spotted her skipping out of
that restaurant. We followed her, and her precious Clive.
Gerry had a word with him. People easily get the jitters
when they're up to no good. He soon spilled the beans, her
name, where she lived. My, wasn't she surprised when I
phoned and suggested we meet! Always an impulsive girl,
Amanda, ready for any adventure. Liked the idea of down
by the old gravel-pits—seemed to think she was in a movie,
the stupid bitch.'

She had put real spitting venom into the last words.

Dorothea felt the surge of an emotion which was neither
fear nor panic. Hatred. Long-buried hatred. Her eyes blazed
and her body moved.

The gun came down smartly, and stung her arm, sending
her back in her seat, wincing with pain. Yet she got out what
she wanted to say.

'Mandy didn't have to die...'

'She'd have died anyway—from that cancer.' Queenie
dismissed Amanda. 'But wasn't that a lucky break for me?
When I read what the doctor said at the inquest...'

'She mightn't have had cancer,' Dorothea found herself
saying through clenched teeth.

'What's it matter? She died, didn't she?'

'I want to know how,' said Dorothea, putting her fingers
on the open gash and squeezing hard.

'You'll get another of the same if you don't keep still,
duckie. Your old mate Amanda was sitting there in her car

scribbling away for dear life... Now, isn't that a happy phrase? We'd parked a good ways off, and crept up on her. This little chap—' she curled strong fingers round it affectionately—'can be most persuasive. Gerry helped her wandering feet. Such dear little pointed heels she'd on, they marked the ground nicely. One push and she was in. Never gave a holler. Guess she knew nobody'd hear... A good sprinkling of gravel soon covered our tracks, and we scarpered damn quick, I can tell you. It was cold enough to freeze the balls of—' She leered at Dorothea. 'I forgot, you never liked expressions like that.'

'She was writing to me,' said Dorothea stubbornly, 'she didn't know about the other thing. You were the malignancy.'

'Gee, don't you know the long words! That was a great letter she was writing, pity most of it had to go... But what we left did the trick. So she was writing to you? You do seem to keep cropping up in my affairs. But this is the last time, I kid you not. I never liked you. Playing at being Miss Prim, with all your airs and graces, looking down on the baddies from your great height of maidenly modesty... Now I know you were just muck like the others, rolling around on Larry's rug in the basement with your knickers round your ankles... Give us another cuppa—it's about all you're fit for...'

Dorothea's hand shook as she lifted the teapot. Why should Queenie's contempt hurt so much more than the blows had done? All the terrible shame she felt rushed in hot blood to burn in her cheeks, yet she poured out Queenie's cup steadily, concentrating only on the simple task. I'll see her in hell... Words she didn't know, feelings she daren't recognize...

Queenie pulled the cup over to her edge of the table, put in milk, two spoonfuls of sugar.

'Ruins the teeth my ma used to say, but I got me a new set since then.' She bared them at Dorothea in a repellent grin.

'So, Dorothea Lingard, you and Larry left me to burn to death.'

Startled by the vicious change in tone, Dorothea burst out: 'He didn't know...'

'Ah, but you did. How come?' The snake's head thrust itself forward, the narrowed eyes black slits.

When Dorothea at last spoke it was as if she was in a dream. The everyday things in the kitchen around her had faded into nothingness.

'We heard a noise upstairs. Larry said, let's get out of here. He was rolling up the rug. I'd left my coat on the banister of the stair. I went to get it and I heard your voice. I thought you were talking to yourself like you did when you walked up and down between the desks. I stopped and listened. I couldn't help myself. It was only a minute, and when I got back to the basement Larry was at the door to the yard but he'd forgotten to take off the kettle... I saw the spark run along the frayed wire... I ran out after Larry... I was in a panic. I thought you'd come down and catch us. I didn't want... I couldn't face...' She stopped, her eyes wide and blank. Now it was out. As if the curtains in her mind had finally been swept aside and she could see clearly how it had been, that overwhelming childish dread of being discovered in a shameful situation. She'd been pulling her underclothes on as she ran, desperately fastening the buttons of her blouse, her coat thrown over her shoulders, out into the loading bay.

'For Christ's sake, hurry.' Larry's voice. He'd locked the door behind them, breathed a sigh of relief when they were in the road.

And later, when the full magnitude of their crime—for so Dorothea saw it—hit them both, he'd made her promise, for his sake, never to tell...

Slowly now she came back to her familiar kitchen, and to the devil that sat in it.

'Who was it?' she asked dully.

'As if you cared. You thought it was me. You hated me, and you left me in a burning building, Dorothea Lingard.' Queenie was enjoying herself. 'Now you can light me a cigarette for old times' sake.' She pushed case and lighter from her bag across the table, raising the gun slightly as she did so.

Dorothea's fingers fumbled. She'd never tasted tobacco before. If I could only jab this flame into that hateful face... But Queenie was smiling, drawing back as if in anticipation of such a move. She took the lighted cigarette, struck it in the corner of her mouth, and returned the case and lighter to the bag. She breathed out smoke into Dorothea's eyes.

'Who was it, you asked... You're not going to live, so what the hell does it matter? Gerry's wife, of course, the real one, the one from Newcastle. Always the proper gentleman, Gerry, he'd the habit of marrying them. And wife number one, she found out about the other one, see? She was going to blow the gaff, and our gallant Major couldn't stand for that, could he? Get rid of her for me, Queenie, he says, good old resourceful Queenie. Meet her in the office late at night when there's no one there, and pay her off. Well, she and I were having a bit of a barney when I got a whiff of that smoke coming up from the basement. She smelt it too, I guess, and went all hysterical, so I clocked her one to shut her up and she struck her stupid head on the filing cabinet and was out cold...'

I don't want to listen to this, thought Dorothea. I don't want to hear about that poor woman, but I've got to keep Queenie talking. So she said:

'Why'd they think it was you?'

'Ah, that's where I was smart. I reckoned she looked like me, same size and about my age. Come to think of it, I'd felt like killing her when she was whining on about Gerry... Anyway, her coat and mine, they were hung up together. She'd a jumper and skirt on like me. I just grabbed my coat and flung it down on her, slipped off my bracelet and shoved it under the coat. It was easy as pie... Only took a coupla seconds...' Queenie was casual, contemptuous even. 'I left my handbag where it was on my desk, took hers and her coat, and was off down the stairs before you could say Jack Robinson. I had the keys to the front door, see? I'd let her in, and me and Gerry, we were the only ones knew she'd come. How'd we to know you two love-sick dummies were canoodling down in the basement?' She broke off, her eyes glinting with anger, the trouble those two had made for her erupting freshly in her mind.

Dorothea saw the danger, flinched from it.

'Did you really think you'd get away with it?' She felt she was talking like a character, saying lines that had been written for her as if in a television script, her lips moving mechanically. Anything to stay Queenie's hand.

The diversion worked. Queenie shrugged. 'What if I hadn't? If they'd discovered the body was really Rosa's? Oh, I'd have faked amnesia, said I couldn't remember rushing out, picking up the wrong things, losing my bracelet... I was in ever such a panic, Sergeant, poor little me caught up in a fire like that, all I thought of was getting away from the place.' She grinned. 'I can play the helpless ninny too when I know it's necessary. And them that thinks you've got to plan murder, they've got it all wrong. You take opportunity by the foreskin... Sorry, ducks, don't I mean forelock? You got to take your chances. That's what happens in business, that's what pays off...'

Her laugh was the scrape of metal on slate.

'Of course I knew Gerry wanted her dead,' she went on. 'I'd seen it in his face when he talked about her, but he lacked the killing instinct. Suited him down to the ground, though, once it was done. She'd no folks, see, up there in Newcastle—nor anywhere else for that matter. Rosa'd been an au pair in some big house when Gerry met her, a German refugee or something. Jewish, I suppose, though I never bothered to find out. When I broke the news to him ever so gently a few weeks later that it was her that was gone and not me, he hadn't a leg to stand on. He'd no alibi for that night, see? And he knew I could stir up a nice little scandal if it suited me. He hadn't come into his money then and he'd have been reduced to the ranks with a vengeance. Not the man to stand that, my Gerry... A few anonymous letters to the other bitch he was living with, and she got the wind up and ran out on him... Clever old Queenie, eh? Off to the States to make her fortune! Why the hell am I telling you all this?'

Because you're boasting, thought Dorothea. Her own mind was clear. She'd never known such clarity. The telling of her shameful secret even to such as the obscene creature in front of her had acted like an explosion, tearing out memories, shredding the past, letting in the light.

I'm cleverer than she is, Dorothea's thoughts were racing, I always was. What's the point of my careful upbringing, my good education, the teaching of my parents, if I can't concentrate the whole in one great effort to defeat a monster like Queenie? Her brain moved, clicking things into place, linking the circuits like a computer, searching for an answer.

'You can't kill me,' she said, looking straight into the black, hateful eyes she remembered so well, the eyes that had scoured her schoolgirl soul and found the flaw. 'They'll know it was you who did it.'

'You're on a loser there, kiddo.' Queenie's head turned to look round the tidy kitchen but her right hand was firm, her thumb on the trigger. 'I've read about places like New-town. A lot of yobbos about, aren't there? Old women get coshed for their pensions, burglaries are run of the mill. What's another suburban housewife done in for the cash in her home, sweet home? All right, you surprised one, what'd happen? A battering to death, that's all. Happens all the time. Of course I won't use little Jimmy here—' she stroked the automatic with her red-tipped fingers—'that would be stupid. They don't use guns, your local creeps. They use the fist or the blunt instrument, whatever comes to hand.' Her eyes flickered around. 'Those knives look sharp, now...'

Despite all effort, Dorothea looked, and her heart quailed.

Knives she couldn't stand, the abrasion of flesh, the slicing, the running blood...

Queenie cocked her head, considering. Clichés were in her mind as they always had been because clichés, as they were called, inevitably held truth.

'The chummies who busted in here to make a few bucks out of the odd bit of silver, or a TV set they could hawk, they'd not have much to lose if they just hit hard and asked questions afterwards... Too bad you'd a thin skull. Now what would they hit you with?'

She got up from her chair and walked over to the wastebin, keeping the gun trained on Dorothea. 'Now here's a thing. A handy mallet. Looks heavy enough to crack a head open.' She brought it back to her place at the table. 'You see, Dottie Dorothea—wasn't that a hell of a name they gave you?—it's got to look it's for real. Like Amanda, and poor old Larry, and now Mrs Copeland...' She spread wide her fingers, spatulate as Dorothea remembered them. 'Just another victim of youthful violence that's the scourge of the 'eighties. Yes, this mallet will do nicely.'

This is not a woman sitting there, thought Dorothea, for all her expensive clothes and her shining new teeth; this is a creation of the devil. She is without morals, without compassion, she acts like she does because she was ill-made in the first place. I've always known it. She is the representation of evil my parents warned me existed, and I never believed them. She is the devil in the world they told me I must fight and I thought they meant drinking, and dancing, and what I did with Larry. But it wasn't that, it was deeper, more terrible.

She no longer felt she had any body even to feel pain; she was all mind and instinct. These she harnessed.

'You can't kill me,' she repeated, 'because I've already told Mr Kemp all about you. He will know. If they find me dead, they'll know it was you.'

Queenie's eyes were on her. To Dorothea they seemed lidless, like a serpent's.

'What's this Kemp man, then?'

'I've told him all about you. About Amanda seeing you. That you weren't dead. That you'd married Major Bulett and were back in England. And he knows about the fire and the cover-up with the insurance company. If I'm found dead Mr Kemp will know who did it. He'll come after you and the Major. You'll not escape British justice, either of you.' Dorothea's voice was not her own. It was as if the words came from some other source than her aching body.

Queenie threw back her head and laughed, a harsh, mirthless sound that splintered the air between them.

'You never told your lawyer pal any such shit. He knows nothing. He's blundering in the dark. You're the crafty one, I'll say that for you, trying that one on. But it won't wash, dearie. Sure, you saw him yesterday. I watched the pair of you, helping you with the shopping, wasn't he? But wouldn't there have been a rumpus by now if you'd spilled the beans like you say? Your Charley'd have known all about it last night, and they'd both be round here now like guardian angels looking out for their little pet. And what's happened in that office of Gillorns, solicitors of Newtown? Why, life goes on as if there wasn't any such thing as a murder plot. No stunning revelations from your murky past. They're too concerned with making money, duckie, ringing up the shekels in their till with all those lovely properties being bought, bless 'em. They're not out to interfere with rich clients like Queenie Bulett.'

It had been many years since Dorothea had listened properly to what her brain told her; there had always been a mist in the way. Now the mist had gone.

Lies, she thought. I'll beat her at her own game, and with her weapons. 'I didn't mean I'd actually told Mr Kemp,' she said, 'but I've written it all down for him and he'll know where to find it. And, anyway,' she added, heaping Pelion upon Ossa, lies upon lies, 'Charley will be here soon. He said he'd be home by half past two.' She looked meaningfully at the clock, its hands at twenty-five past.

Queenie didn't even glance at it.

'Charley is me darlin', me darlin', me darlin',' she crooned, leaning back and tilting her head. She took a deep draw on her cigarette, and let smoke filter from her nostrils. 'Your darlin' Charley's over the hills and far away. Gone out into the wilds of Hertfordshire to look at that manor of mine... I went there once, see, when I was a kid on an orphanage outing. Yeah, you may well stare... That's what me dear old ma did with me when she was off with her feller—put me in an orphanage, like the sticks of furniture she'd thrown on the scrapheap. But I seen that place, all them green lawns and flowers...' Queenie was all Cockney now, back where the dream had begun. 'They'd put us lot in any old field with the long grass and thistles, and we'd to bring our own bread-and-scrape—with jam on because it were a Sunday. But I had a dekko at them lords and ladies with their parasols and their tea-party, and I says to myself: 'Queenie, one day you'll be back and it won't be in no smelly meadow you'll eat.'

'Charley will come any minute now,' Dorothea repeated stubbornly. 'You're lying.'

Queenie put on her posh voice: 'I'd like Mr Copeland to meet me at Broxburn Hall, shall we say two-thirty? That lah-di-dah young lady in reception and me, we had quite a chat. Told me all about the staff meeting, business as usual in Gillorns, no panic about little Mrs Copeland being in

danger! And that nice Mr Kemp? Oh, he's half-asleep listening to them all talk, and then she goes and gets Charley
to the phone, and, yes, dearie, I spoke with him. He'll be
there by now. Conscientious chap, I guess, he'll not give up
easily. Take him more than a coupla hours.' Her eyes were
flickering round the kitchen again. 'It was a nice try, kiddo.
You've got more spunk than I thought you'd have, but no
knight's gonna ride in here on a white charger so you might
as well forget it.'

But Dorothea sensed anger beneath the contempt, and
colour had risen under Queenie's sallow skin. Dorothea kept
silent.

'You left me to burn, Dorothea Lingard. Why shouldn't
you go the same way? An unfortunate fire... That's what
they call poetic justice, ain't it? Have you got a chip-pan?
Every suburban housewife has a chip-pan.'

She got up and went over to the stove, keeping the gun
steady. 'Electric, huh? Well, it was gas put the skids under
your buddy, Larry. I'd be a real dope if I tried that twice.'

She broke off, stood over Dorothea and pressed the cold
metal of the gun against her ear. 'First, what's this crap
about writing things down?'

Dorothea didn't turn round. Instead, she fixed her eyes
on the slow hands of the clock, the blue and white Dutch-
looking clock she'd bought to match the table and chairs.
This is my centre, she thought, this is my kitchen, these ob-
jects are mine and I'll defend them with all my will. Already Queenie's confused; she's no longer the cool,
calculating beast she was an hour ago. She'd talked of killing, of blunt instruments, of the knives on the wall, now
she's considering fire... But the lies had stayed her hand.

'It's all written down in my diary,' she said, 'and that
won't be destroyed even if you burn the house to the
ground.'

'Where's this fucking diary?' Queenie spat at her, grind-
ing the point of the gun against her temple. Dorothea closed

her eyes. If it had been a knife, she thought in despair, if she cut ... But the black shining thing, what did it mean? One piercing shot and then oblivion.

'It's at my mother's house,' she said calmly, 'where you'll never find it.' Forgive me, Mother, she told that long-dead and only recently loved figure. Their house had been sold years ago. Forgive my lies, she prayed, there's a time for lying as there's a time for truth. God, make her believe my lies.

This time the blow was sharper. It sent her head down on the white table-top and she kept it there, thankful for the coolness of the plastic against her burning forehead.

TWENTY-THREE

STAFF MEETINGS at Gillorns came about every three months, and were informal affairs during which topics of concern to all in the office were freely discussed, from changes in interest rates and professional charges to the kind of biscuits preferred with their coffee. The meetings were held in the typists' room since it was the largest in the building, refreshments were provided but no alcohol—Kemp didn't believe in taking informality that far—and time restricted to one hour of the lunch-break.

Today it had started at a quarter to one but was still dragging on at two o'clock, mainly because Kemp had been far from his usual brisk, businesslike self. He had to be roused several times from what looked like torpor.

'You asleep, Lennox?' whispered young Belchamber at one point.

'Just thinking... Sorry, everybody. What were we talking about?'

'The collection for Nick's leaving present,' Michael Cantley prompted. 'Seemed a good opportunity while he's out finishing up his cases in Court. He's no loss to us but we'll have to make a gesture.'

'Put the usual list round the office. Whatever you get, I'll double it. Solidarity in the profession, you know,' Kemp replied listlessly. It was generous on his part, he knew, but he'd not have Nick Stoddart sniping back at the firm. 'Now, I hope there's nothing else? Right. Then we'll close.'

Back in his own office he threw himself heavily into his chair. Thinking, he'd said. What good was thinking? He'd spent most of last night thinking, and got nowhere. He'd become obsessed with this happening—it wasn't even a proper case any more—out of the past, obsessed with facts that lay in forgotten papers, and with people he'd never met; some he would never meet, like Larry Lanscombe and the unknown woman who'd died in the fire.

Even Elvira was cross with him. Instead of concentrating on the work to hand—of which there was plenty—he had her running around for old records, phoning the Edmonton Fire Service, the Coroner's Office for the district, pestering them to open files twenty years out of date. It would take time, they grumbled, and she in her turn grumbled at him...

The telephone buzzed at his elbow. Lisa at reception. 'It's a Mrs McIlvey on the line for you, Mr Kemp. Says it isn't urgent but she'd like a word if you were free.'

'That's all right, Liz, I'll take the call.'

Grace McIlvey's voice was hesitant. 'Mr Kemp? I'm not bothering you, am I?'

'Of course not. How's Ted?'

'Better, thanks. I'll not keep you, Mr Kemp. It was just that Milly and me went through the things in poor Larry's house, like I said. There weren't much but I came across some letters of his mother's. She'd kept a lot of stuff and Larry'd never got round to throwing them out. She'd kept birthday cards and Christmas cards like some folks do... Sure I'm not bothering you?' She was getting breathless.

'Not at all. Take your time, Grace.'

'Well, I remember you asking about Larry's girls—did he ever bring them home—and I'd said there was one. The name had gone right out of my head when you asked me, Mr Kemp. It was that long ago she was spoke of. But I found a Christmas card she'd sent to Mrs Lanscombe, and her name was on it. Dorothea. I knew it were a pretty name, and that was it, Dorothea. She worked in that office at Higgs, that's how she came to go out with Larry. Are you still there, Mr Kemp?'

'Yes, Grace, I am.'

'It seemed important to you at the time you asked, so when I found the card I says to Ted I'd call you, and Ted says yes I should. You did want to know, didn't you?'

'Thank you. Yes, I did want to know and I'm grateful for your trouble.'

'Got to go now, Mr Kemp. We've not got a phone and I'm in a box. Just thought I'd let you know...'

Kemp put down the phone, and stared at it.

He struck his fist on his head. 'Oh, you bloody fool,' he told himself, 'you slow-thinking idiot...' Of course that was the link, the one he'd been looking for. He should have known... Snatches of conversation came back to him: 'Mandy and I, we started work together...' and, more recently: 'There was this dreadful shabby office...'

Then the hatred in Dorothea's voice. The name Queenie. That name was linked too with Amanda. 'She had this crazy story, that Queenie was still alive.'

But why had Dorothea never mentioned where she and Mandy had worked? More to the point, why had Charles never mentioned it? Stoddart had said Dorothea helped with the typing of the court case, she'd shredded the missing documents—the ones with Larry Lanscombe's name on them? But Stoddart had never said she'd worked at Higgs, and he would have told had he known. He'd been puzzled by what he thought of as her fall from grace... So he didn't know. Dorothea Lingard had known all about the fire at Higgs, and Larry's part in it, long before she saw those papers.

And Charley must have known.

Kemp was swept by anger. He lifted the phone and jabbed a button. 'Charles!' he yelled into the mouthpiece. 'I want you in my room, this minute!'

At the other end, Lambert held the phone away from his ear.

'It's Tony. Charles isn't in right now.'

'Where the hell is he?'

'Gone out to that Broxburn place.'

'What the devil for?'

'I say, Lennox, keep your hair on. The client asked him to meet her there this afternoon . . .'

'What client?'

'The one who came in yesterday,' explained Lambert patiently, 'the one who wants to make a quick purchase of Broxburn Hall. She suggested Charles went out there to have a good look round the property so that he can check the draft contract when it comes in. She wants no time wasted. Seemed a good idea to me . . . Charles is an old hand at spotting anything from quasi-easements to dubious drains . . . By the way, she seemed to know you.'

'Who does?' Kemp barked.

'This client. She recognized you in the car park yesterday when you were at your car with Mrs Copeland.'

'What was she like?'

'Who, Mrs Copeland? Sorry, Lennox, but you're getting me all confused. The client, you mean? I've got her name somewhere on this desk. A Mrs Frazer. Not young, but had style. Striking-looking woman. Something odd about her voice. Mid-Atlantic, I'd say of her accent, but she wasn't out of the top drawer . . .'

'Is there a telephone out there?' Kemp broke in.

'At Broxburn Hall? Shouldn't think so. The place has been empty for months.'

'Who's the agent?'

'Carstairs. What's going on, Lennox?' Tony jumped as the banging-down of the receiver hit his eardrum.

Kemp was frantically calling Carstairs Estate Agency.

'That name doesn't appear to be on our mailing list, Mr Kemp, but of course we've sent out a considerable number of brochures on the property. It's a very desirable place . . .'

'Spare me the hype. Is this Mrs Frazer on your books as a serious buyer or not? Has she been into your office?'

'I'll inquire.'

'Don't take your time about it,' Kemp snapped. Nearly half past two. How long would it have taken Charles to get out there, and just who, or what, had been waiting for him?

'The personification of evil,' Dorothea had said. Where had he felt that presence? Outside the Inkerman Arms, the flicker of a red skirt . . .

'Nobody in this agency has seen or heard of a Mrs Frazer. Do I understand your clerk is out at Broxburn Hall now?'

'Yes.'

'Well, he has no right to be there. No keys to the property have been released. I've got them here in my hand, Mr Kemp.'

Kemp stamped out to reception.

'She called during the lunch-time meeting,' Lisa told him, 'Yes, I'm sure it was the lady who came in yesterday. I recognized her voice. She wanted a message given to Charley—to Mr Copeland. Said she was going ahead with the purchase of Broxburn Hall, and she'd like him to go out there right away. She hung on while I had a word with him. You remember, I interrupted the meeting . . .'

'Yes, I remember.' Charley had got up and gone to the phone, had come back looking pleased with himself.

'I heard him tell her he'd meet her there about two-thirty or nearer three if the meeting finished late . . . Seemed all right to me. Whatever's the matter, Mr Kemp?' Lisa had looked at his face, which was grim.

He strode back into his office but didn't sit down. He walked up and down, trying to think, trying to pull the threads together.

It all went back to Higgs Electric. Three of the names he knew were working there at the time of the fire: Larry Lanscombe, Amanda Richards, Dorothea Lingard, and the unknown woman who had died.

'*But Mandy had this crazy tale ... that Queenie was still alive.*'

Kemp ran for his car.

It wasn't Charley they were after. Charley hadn't worked at Higgs. The other three had, and two of them were dead. Charley was just a stalking-horse.

As he raced the engine, Kemp looked at his watch. Getting on for three o'clock. The time he'd wasted... He swung the car out into the main road, swearing at the traffic jam.

TWENTY-FOUR

QUEENIE HAD REGAINED her composure, and the upper hand she'd always considered her due. Silly to lose her temper with this milksop of a creature. No one in a long time had had the cheek to stand up to Queenie, and Queenie's luck would hold.

It was three o'clock but she would work quickly from now on. She'd already put the pan on the stove, the ring was glowing red beneath it. She went over to the table and sat down again opposite the slumped figure.

Dorothea raised her head, and looked at her from a stony face streaked with blood.

'Still got those freckles, duckie? You're a bit blotchy. Never mind, a spot of hot oil will soon take them off. See, I got the ladle handy...'

'I'm not going to do what you want.' Dorothea by now knew what it was like to feel mutinous. 'Whatever you do to me...'

'Serves you right for talking about that bloody diary—if it exists. You just make a phone call to your mum, and tell her to post it to the address I'll give you. Tell her quietly, now, no fooling around. I'll be there beside you, holding the phone.' Queenie gave a sigh of exasperation. 'I'm fast running out of patience with you, my girl.'

'I won't do it.' Dorothea put her hands on the table, gripping its top. When she'd fallen on it she'd felt it move on the polished linoleum tiles. It was the bane of Charley's life, that table. The chairs don't fit in properly under it, he'd said, and it's never steady. He'd wanted something more solid, like stripped pine even though that was more expensive. But Dorothea had liked it the moment she'd seen it in the shop, blue and white, the steel legs of the chairs gleaming like silver. It's cleaner and brighter than wood, she'd said, and they'd bought the set; but it was true the table wobbled.

Queenie's eyes were sliding sideways towards the stove.

'Save you a lot of pain, kiddo, if you do as I say... Otherwise there'll be brown splotches on your face that ain't freckles.'

She gestured with the gun. Dorothea was getting sick and tired of that gun.

'C'mon, upsi-daisy... Move your ass into the hall and get on that phone to your mum. Tell her where to send the package. Me and the Major, we'll see to it at the other end.'

Dorothea felt the table move ever so slightly as she tightened her grasp on it. She shook her head slowly from side to side, taking her time.

'You'll never get that diary, Queenie. You can kill me but you'll be caught. It's all there about you in my diary. You'll never be the lady of the manor anywhere. They'll hunt you down, you and your precious Major.'

Dorothea felt the hard steel of the chair leg against her knees, and knew it was edge to edge with the table leg; that was the reason the chairs wouldn't fit in properly. She could almost feel the strength of the steel flowing into her body.

There was real fury now in Queenie's eyes. She was crouching forward like a black spider, willing to wound yet afraid to strike.

Despite the menace, Dorothea felt something like exultation. She believes the lie, she thought, she believes there really is a diary. She daren't kill me unless she's sure of getting hold of it.

'And it's no use you getting me to phone my mother because she isn't in. This is her day for helping at the Save the Children shop, and they're not on the phone,' Dorothea went on evenly. How easily the lies came once you'd started!

Irresolution crossed Queenie's face. She was a creature of instant decision and quick actions. She despised those who fumbled, people who were in two minds... Now she was vacillating, and it showed.

Dorothea saw that her moment had come.

She heaved herself up in one swift movement, and pushed, hands and feet braced to take the strain. The table slid forward, catching Queenie full in the midriff so that she staggered and fell as her chair went over. The gun flew up out of her fingers as Dorothea ran to the sink. She wrung out the washing-up cloth and used it to lift the pan of oil which was just beginning to show a faint blue haze.

Calmly, almost casually, she threw the contents at Queenie who was on the floor, struggling to raise herself out of the tangle of chair legs.

It was the sound of Queenie's screams that Kemp heard as he burst open the door of the house.

Dorothea was standing by the sink, her dark blue eyes blazing. Behind her in the washing-up bowl a useless black object lay helpless among the bubbles.

TWENTY-FIVE

'NOT ONE OF MY most successful cases,' Lennox Kemp observed ruefully, rubbing his cheek where the scratches still showed red after two weeks. 'I should have found out about that link a lot earlier...'

'But you got there in time, thank God.' Charles Copeland replenished Kemp's glass. They were in the sitting-room, and it was late at night. Dorothea had already gone to bed.

'The doctor says she has to rest. Otherwise she's going to be all right. I still can't get over how she stood up to that—that fiend.'

'Emotion has a strength that's more than physical, stronger sometimes than either instinct or reason. Dorothea's emotions go very deep, back to her childhood, the formation of her character, the standards she was taught.' Kemp sighed. It was hard to put into words what he only vaguely understood himself. 'She saw it as a struggle, if you like, between good and evil,' he went on, almost as if talking to himself. 'The power of darkness against the power of light...'

He touched his cheek again.

'Queenie—that fiend, as you call her—certainly fought like an alleycat, and I've got the marks to prove it. The burns will heal but I don't suppose her soul ever will.'

'What can she be charged with?'

'Well, she's already been charged with causing grievous bodily harm to your wife, Charles. As to the other murders—for murders they were—there'll have to be a full investigation. A long, wearisome process...'

Kemp picked up his glass.

'And that Major?' asked Charles.

'I can't help feeling a touch of pity for him. He's tied to a tiger, and well he knows it. She's already full of wild accusations against him. Their two separate stories will tangle themselves into a fine knot, and they'll go down together.'

'Dorothea will have to go to court?' Charles sounded apprehensive.

Kemp laughed, then sobered hastily; his view of Dorothea was not the same as her husband's.

'She will have to testify, yes. But don't look so worried, Charles, your Dorothea will do it with gusto.'

Kemp nearly added that anyone who could throw a panful of boiling oil in someone's face, no matter how rightful the cause, was unlikely to be intimidated by Counsel for the Defence.

He had not said as much to Charles Copeland; it would take time for Charley to adjust, and perhaps come to a fresh perception of his dearest Dorothea despite having been married to her for over twenty years.

SHANNON DELL

First Time in Paperback

Destiny of Death

A LUIS MENDOZA MYSTERY

The weather was as gray and nasty as Lieutenant Luis Mendoza's caseload....

A nice young man is helping little old ladies with their groceries...then stealing their Social Security; an enormous "ape man" with a face like King Kong is robbing liquor stories; "Jack the Stripper" is leaving gas station registers empty...and the attendants naked.

An ordinary old man appears to commit suicide; a pretty Hispanic woman is killed and ethnic tensions are ready to explode; a little girl is mutilated; a cop is fatally shot.

Between the weather and the crime wave, Lieutenant Luis Mendoza—the family-man cop—finds shelter at home—knowing that even violence on the streets of Los Angeles eases up...eventually.

Dell Shannon "is the reigning doyenne of the U.S. police procedural."
—*Kirkus Reviews*

HOOKY GETS
THE WOODEN SPOON
LAURENCE MEYNELL

First Time in Paperback

HOOKY HEFFERMAN WAS MUCH BETTER AT GETTING GIRLS IN TROUBLE THAN OUT OF IT.

His passion for the fair sex and English pubs aside, he had been known to solve a crime or two as a private investigator, profiting from the idiocies of this comic adventure called life.

Now he's been hired to find a rebellious, poor little rich girl who has taken up with some unsavory characters. Dad isn't comfortable swimming the murky waters of London's underground. Hooky, however, feels quite at home.

He's never minded helping out a pretty face—and Virginia Chanderley is that—but young and angry, she's also easy prey for a professional crook planning to steal a priceless painting. In fact, lovely Virginia has got herself into more trouble than even Hooky Hefferman—London P.I. and soldier of fortune—knows quite how to handle.

"Laurence Meynell had a gift for creating recognizable characters and ingenious plots."
—*The Independent*

MYSTERY **WORLDWIDE LIBRARY**
™

THE CRUEL MOTHER

A MEG HALLORAN MYSTERY

JANET LAPIERRE

WERE THEY CAPTIVES BECAUSE OF SOME MOUNTAIN MAN'S FANTASY? OR SOMETHING COMPLETELY UNCONNECTED?

Meg Halloran's romantic getaway with longtime love, policeman Vince Gutierrez looks less appealing when Vince reluctantly introduces the third member of their party, his spike-haired, foul-mouthed niece, Cass.

An accident with another car abruptly ends their plans. Then Meg and Cass are inexplicably abducted, held in a secluded wilderness cabin in Idaho's panhandle.

Meg desperately seeks answers—and a means of escape—unaware her fate lies with strangers: a terminally-ill sixties radical who recently confessed to murder; his wife, emerging from seclusion to reunite the dying man with their young daughter; and a lawyer, calculating one of the biggest scores of his circumspect career....